Evie and Maryam's Family Tree

GUPPY BOOKS

JANEEN HAYAT

Evie and Maryam's Family Tree

GUPPY BOOKS

EVIE AND MARYAM'S FAMILY TREE
is a GUPPY BOOK

First published in the UK in 2025 by
Guppy Books,
Bracken Hill,
Cotswold Road,
Oxford OX2 9JG

Text copyright © Janeen Hayat, 2025

ISBN: 978 1916558 410

1 3 5 7 9 10 8 6 4 2

Papers used by Guppy Books are from well-managed
forests and other responsible sources.

MIX
Paper | Supporting
responsible forestry
FSC® C171272

GUPPY PUBLISHING LTD Reg. No. 11565833

A CIP catalogue record for this book is
available from the British Library.

Typeset in 11/19 pt Minion Pro by Falcon Oast Graphic Art Ltd
Printed and bound in Great Britain by CPI Books Ltd

To Dad, who gave me the story, and Mom,
who gave me the pen

LONDON, UK

PRESENT DAY

1. Maryam

Maryam's right foot tapped like a woodpecker. 'Hassan! Hurry *up!*' she called to the bedroom.

She had just said it two minutes ago and was getting increasingly anxious. Hassan didn't answer, but Nani stirred in her battered, brown leather armchair, asleep in the living room. Nani woke up before dawn when Maryam's parents left to open their shop, but needed a snooze by the time Maryam got out of bed.

Maryam went into her comfort zone for when she was stressed: drawing noses. She sat at the dining room table, her elbows drawn close to her to avoid bumping into one of the many piles of envelopes, receipts and papers stacked on the embroidered tablecloth. She sketched an old man's nose, a long and dangly nose hair creeping out

3

of a nostril, but quickly erased it in disgust – too weird for anyone to see. The whole corner of the page now had noses of various shapes and sizes, from bulbous to pointed.

She pushed her glasses up on her own nose. Everywhere she looked in her small flat, there were *things*: papers, boxes, ring binders. She snaked her line of sight around these to the digital clock on the sideboard: 8.34 a.m.

It was the same most mornings: Maryam woke to the sound of Hassan snoring in the bunk bed below, got dressed, ate a slice of toast with butter and sugar, and then waited for her brother with her shoes on and her back-pack zipped.

She breathed out with a huff and perfected a nostril.

The noses were strange, but not as strange as the paper they were doodled on. The yellowed, lined page was in a faded red folder that she'd discovered in a box in Nani's bedroom. She liked to rummage around in that room – often she'd find nothing but photos she'd already seen dozens of times, but sometimes she'd stumble upon long-forgotten treasures. The folder was entirely ordinary, with two pockets on the inside, and a label written in Urdu on the outside. But the page itself was full of complete nonsense. It read:

Uvri Jrwzr,

Z yfgv pfl riv nvcc reu kyrk pfl'mv svve rscv kf uvtzgyvi kyzj cvkkvi.

The rest of the page was the same – full of unpronounce-able words that barely looked like words at all. And behind that page, there were about ten more like it. It was, by far, the most mysterious thing she'd ever found in Nani's collection.

Maryam wished her Urdu was better, but although she could make out some of the letters on the cover, she couldn't get the words. What was strange was that the nonsense words on the pages in the folder were definitely not Urdu. They weren't written in Arabic letters like the label, but in the same letters used for English. She looked across the room at Nani, dozing peacefully. She'd ask her about it after school.

Finally, there was movement in the corridor.

'Sorry, sorry, sorry, sorry, sorry,' Hassan said as he bounded out of their room. It wasn't completely his fault he always slept in. He was up late doing homework every night because he was trying really hard to do well in his exams. They were still three years away for Maryam, but already loomed large in her imagination. 'You ready?'

5

Maryam nodded and shoved the folder in her bag. She and Hassan stepped into the living room and each gave Nani a kiss on the forehead. She rolled over and said a sleepy, 'Bye bye, my loves,' with a wave.

Maryam skipped down the steps of their block of flats, running across the courtyard.

'Hassan, I am always, *always*, the latest one.'

'Yeah, but you're the cleverest one, so it doesn't matter!' He yanked on her plait and opened the gate.

Hassan said the last word 'maa-uh', dropping his Ts like he'd started doing recently. It riled Maryam up, but she couldn't stay annoyed at him when he was in a happy mood. They turned down the high street and marched with a stream of other children going to St Mary's Secondary School. Maryam recognised some of them – even knew their names – but she knew they either wouldn't know her name, or would pretend not to if she said hello.

'Hey, Hassan,' she said, almost jogging to keep up with him now. 'I found something weird in Nani's room.'

'Is that news?' he asked, without breaking his stride. 'There's all kinds of sus stuff in that room.'

'No, I mean, like, *interesting*,' she said. 'It's this folder with a bunch of letters in it, but they're written in complete gibberish.'

'Um, that's called Urdu,' Hassan said.

'Shut up, I know what Urdu looks like,' Maryam said, frustrated. 'It's the same *letters* as English, but the words are completely unintelligible. Like, all consonants and no vowels.'

'Maybe Nani had a Russian pen pal,' Hassan replied. They were approaching the school gates, the stream of teenagers in school uniform getting thicker.

'I don't think it's Russian,' Maryam said. 'I'll show you at home.'

'Sure, see you later,' he said, and jogged off to the Year Ten door.

'See you,' she said, looking at the clock at the front of the school. 8.47. They were late. Maryam entered the main door, ran upstairs and staggered into the form room, panting for breath. Their teacher, Mr Whipple, sat at his desk while the class chatted loudly. *Whipple Wednesdays.* Regular form time was bad enough – Maryam always sat awkwardly, drawing on her own while the rest of the class joked and got increasingly out of control. But on

Wednesdays, they had to do group work, and it seemed that everyone had someone to pair up with but her.

She entered the room sheepishly and made eye contact with Mr Whipple. He raised his eyebrows disapprovingly and tapped his watch, but then went back to his computer. Her glasses were starting to fog up, and she lingered at the door, wiping them and then flapping her shirt to get some air in. The last thing she wanted was to be the weird, sweaty girl. Being the weird girl was enough.

She settled into her seat at her table, where the others – Ted, Leo and Evie – carried on chatting without acknowledging her. Ted was telling a story about how he'd stolen a bag of crisps from the corner shop while the others leaned in, asking questions in awe. Maryam looked down uncomfortably and thought about her mum, at the till of their shop, and her dad, unpacking boxes in the back room, counting every packet of crisps he put on the shelf.

'It was so easy,' Ted said with a smirk. 'If any of you lot are hungry, just let me know. I might make a little trip back there after school and help myself to a chocolate bar.'

She took out her book and a pen, chewing on the inside

of her cheek in anger. Maryam had noticed her parents'
whispers and furrowed brows the night before – something wasn't going well, although she wasn't sure what.
She thought of Ted, chipping away at what little they had.
She didn't know what shop he'd stolen from, but it didn't
matter. It might as well have been theirs.

'I'm gonna call you "Pincher" from now on,' Leo said.
'Just pinch some sweet chilli crisps for me next time, OK?'

Evie, sitting across from Maryam, rolled her eyes and
said, 'You're so annoying.' Ted and Leo laughed, and Evie
sat back in her seat and examined her fingernails.

The small bit of support took down a barrier in
Maryam's brain. She drew in a sharp breath, held it in her
chest and put her palms flat on the table as she let it out.
She looked at Ted, her cheeks flushed.

'You actually are though,' she said seriously. She hadn't
intended to insert herself into the conversation, her rage
had just sort of taken over her brain and pushed the
words out.

The three stopped talking and looked at each other.

''Scuse me?' Ted asked, chuckling.

'Annoying,' Maryam clarified. Now that she'd spoken

up, she figured she might as well keep going. 'Do you not know that someone owns that shop, and you're stealing from them?'

There was a beat of silence, and then Leo finally said, 'Ooh, sick burn!' in a mocking voice to Ted, who laughed, and then carried on talking. Maryam briefly caught Evie's eye, but she quickly looked away and got up to speak to a friend at another table. Maryam felt partly relieved that it ended there, and partly disappointed that no one could even be bothered to get into an argument with her. She opened her mouth to say something else, but all of the options that ran through her head sounded weak.

Maryam looked down at the blank page in her book and started doodling, trying to move her brain on, trying to distract herself from what had just happened so the tears wouldn't come. But they did, and she felt a fat drop roll under the frame of her glasses down her cheek, which she quickly wiped away. No one at the table seemed to notice, but she knew they'd be talking about her at break, doing mean impersonations. She pretended to need something from her bag, hiding her face under the table for a few moments so she could compose herself. She took out the red folder and pulled out the page she'd been drawing on that morning.

Uvri Jrwzr,

Z yfgv pfl riv nvcc reu kyrk pfl'mv svve rscv kf uvtzgyvi kyzj cvkkvi.

It looked like a greeting, maybe the opening of a letter. It was signed off as:

Pfli wizveu,

Brkyp

Brkyp seemed to be a name, but she'd never heard it before and couldn't begin to pronounce it. What was this doing in Nani's room? Nani would at least be able to read the Urdu label on the front of the folder – maybe that would give her a clue. Suddenly, Mr Whipple was clapping, and the class clapped back, and she shoved the folder back in her bag.

2. Evie

Evie slumped on the sofa, holding one sock and wearing the other, wondering what kind of person would kill a dog. Was it the same kind of person who would kill a human, or would they perhaps be not quite as bad? She needed to understand the villain of the book she was going to write: *Pupslayer*. So far, it was only an idea – a grizzled, small-town detective hunting down a dog murderer. Mum had said it sounded a bit gruesome, but the kids at her school liked gore – just look at the recent obsession with wildlife shows where at least one of the animal cast members got eaten. Evie had read so many detective stories, she was sure she could write one.

'Honestly, Evie! We are late. And you don't even have your socks on!' Her mum, reaching over her shoulder to pick up the remote and turn off the TV, jolted her back to reality.

Mum radiated stress, alternating between scrolling through work emails and asking why Evie and Zac were so slow. She now stood in the doorway to the sitting room, wearing high-heeled boots with her wavy, blondish hair – the same colour as Evie's – tied up in a bun. Evie guessed she had an important meeting. To be fair to Mum, Dad had left early to go to work, and from the way she kept checking her phone and breathing out through puffed cheeks, it seemed that something was going wrong. Still, Evie felt unable to focus on any particular task. She sat up on the sofa, trying to remember what she was supposed to be doing.

'Even Zac is ready. Shouldn't you be setting an example for him and not the other way around?'

If Zac was ready, it was probably because he had put his uniform on over his pyjamas again. But Zac always got away with more because he was five years younger. Evie pulled her second sock on and went hunting for her shoes.

'Oh and Evie, remember to bring a diary to write your

homework down so you can keep track,' Mum called from upstairs. Evie felt her trademark flakiness was getting worse lately – there was just so much to hold in her brain now that she was in secondary school, and random thoughts like ideas for stories or how her thumbnail was peeling off kept crowding out the growing list of things she needed to remember.

She went upstairs to her room and pulled out the tattered red folder she'd found in Gran's house when they had visited last weekend. It had a label on the front that said *Family Recipes* in elegant handwriting, and she'd liked how old it looked and the beauty of the perfect script writing. She had thought it was a bound notebook, but when she opened it now, she found that it was full of loose sheets of paper that came tumbling out. The pages looked old – they were slightly yellowed and greasy looking. But what was really strange was the writing itself. Not only did they look like letters, not recipes, the words weren't like any language she'd ever seen:

Uvri Brkyp,

Z rd jfiip zk yrj krbve dv jf cfex kf nizkv.

Evie looked at the sheet, puzzled. The only other

14

language anyone in her family spoke was French, and as bad as Evie's French was, she could tell this wasn't that. She looked at the few other pages that had fallen out – they were the same. They looked like letters, but was 'Brkyp' a name? The letter was signed off 'Jrwzr'. How could you have a name with no vowels?

Mum flung the door open, Zac's PE bag in her hand. 'Have you seen your brother's sweatshirt?' she asked, starting to empty the drawers.

'No. Weird question, but do you know what this is?' Evie asked, holding up the page. Mum gave it the briefest of glances.

'Evie, if you have spare time, I'd really rather you practised your piano rather than doodle in that note-book.' Mum reached behind the dresser with a sigh. 'You know, Arabella passed her grade four exam last week.' Bella was Mum's model of someone who was going to get into a great university, and Evie was always lagging at least a little bit behind.

Finding the sweatshirt, Mum took a closer look at the page, which Evie still held in front of her. 'No, I've never seen that before. Where did you get it?'

'Gran's house,' Evie said quietly, the piano comment still stinging.

'Well, ask Gran the next time we see her,' Mum said. Evie looked at the page, confused, before closing the folder and shoving it in her backpack.

Outside, Zoe and her little brother Hector were waiting on the other side of the street to join them for the walk to school. Zoe and Evie had gone to primary school together, and their parents were friends too. Along with Bella, their parents called them the Three Amigos even though they were getting a little old for that nickname.

Evie looked at Zoe like a stranger would – she had, suddenly, grown up over the summer holidays. She looked like a teenager, with her combat boots and her dark hair cut in a sharp, chin-length bob. Evie thought how she must look next to her – a head shorter, with frizzy blonde hairs popping out of her high ponytail and sensible Mary-Janes on her feet. Like a child walking to school with her big sister. Evie ran her tongue over the metal bumps of her braces, a nervous habit she'd developed since she got them last month. She slowed her pace down, dropping behind her mum to fall in step with Zoe.

'So, something strange happened this morning,' Evie started right in. Zoe's eyebrows raised expectantly. 'I got this old folder from my gran's house last weekend, and when I opened it today it was full of letters. But they're in a crazy language I've never seen before.' She saw from the lowering of Zoe's eyebrows that she did not find this particularly exciting.

'Hang on,' Evie said, unzipping her bag as they walked and taking the folder out, eager to show Zoe what she meant. She carefully took out the top page, making sure the others didn't blow away. 'Look,' she said, handing it to Zoe.

Slowing her pace down a bit as she inspected it, Zoe wrinkled her nose. 'Who's "Brkyp"?' She said it 'Burkyip', which was also how Evie had been pronouncing it in her head.

'No idea,' Evie said, glad that Zoe saw how odd it was.

'I think it might be Finnish,' Zoe said, scanning the page. 'When we went to Lapland last Christmas, the Finnish words were completely crazy.'

Evie took the page back, carefully tucked it into the folder, and zipped the bag up. Why would Gran have a bunch of letters in Finnish? She started to feel excited at having a mystery to solve. But then she checked herself – she was being childish. Surely Gran had just had a pen pal.

When they got to the gate of the primary school, the boys put their scooters in the rack and Zac gave her an unexpected hug before he ran in without another word. She wondered how much longer he'd want to hug her in public. He could be quite annoying, but she liked his hugs.

'You girls OK from here?' Mum asked. They nodded and Evie's mum squeezed her arm and said, 'Have a great day,' and then, in a lower voice, 'I'm sorry I snapped at you about the piano.'

Evie looked up the hill at the big brick building with teenagers pouring through the gates. 'It's OK,' she said. As she waved goodbye and watched her mum quickly clicking down the pavement in her heels, she felt a little pang that made her want to grab her mum's hand and ask her to come all the way to the gate, like when she was a little kid. She didn't feel ready for a six-period day, or being put in sets, or the feeling that the adults weren't making sure they were OK any more. There was a wildness to secondary school – sometimes, a meanness – that unsettled her.

With relief, Evie remembered it was Whipple Wednesday – extended form lessons that felt less stressful than the subjects they got marked on. She said bye to Zoe as they parted ways in the corridor and Evie walked into Mr Whipple's form room. Bella was already in her seat, and had her arm bent around her paper and her head close to the desk, her long, auburn hair covering her face. She was drawing something in the top margin.

'Hey,' Evie said, hovering next to her seat.

'Hey, Evie,' she said, sitting up, 'check out my drawing.' Bella revealed a cartoonish panda with big, shiny eyes. Bella's freckled nose wrinkled with amusement. 'Look like anyone?' Mr Whipple was a kind teacher, but he did bear a striking resemblance to a panda. He was big, quite hairy, had dark circles around his large, watery eyes, and was often chewing a stick of gum – like bamboo.

'You're mean,' Evie laughed on her way to her own table, where Ted and Leo were deep in football conversation, and Maryam, the fourth person, was late as usual.

Ted lived on Evie's road and they'd known each other forever, but it was only recently that he'd seemed to realise that his dad being an actor on TV made him cool by association. Ted being cool had not had a positive effect on his personality. At the moment he was bragging about how he'd stolen a bag of crisps from the corner shop while Leo, his new lapdog, basically panted his approval. Evie thought of the Ted she'd played with when they were little – who would cry when his mum left the room – and figured he was probably lying.

'You're so annoying,' she muttered, as she often did at Ted.

'You are, actually,' said Maryam, catching Evie off guard. She hadn't noticed Maryam come in, and they all stopped and looked at her. 'Annoying,' she said, looking down at her desk but breathing deeply. Her brown skin had flushed pink. 'Do you not know that someone owns that shop, and you're stealing from them?'

Maryam was new, and a bit weird. She had hardly spoken since the beginning of the school year, didn't seem to have many friends, and always looked slightly dishevelled, like her clothes didn't fit right. Bella had started calling her Wednesday on account of her plaits and sullen look. Why was she choosing this moment to speak up? She now looked over the desk at Evie, her eyes wide with rage and welling with tears, seeming to want Evie to back her up.

Evie refused to be drawn into an argument. She averted her eyes, got up from the table and went back to Bella, kneeling by her seat and giggling over the animal representations she'd done of people in their form. She suggested that Bella do Leo as Ted's pet dog next.

But then Mr Whipple was clapping his hands at the front of the class, and she went back to her seat and clapped back.

3. Amma

Maryam dragged her feet through the door of her flat and plodded into her bedroom, the strangeness of the morning still swirling round her head. Her mum followed her through and lingered in the doorway, but Maryam ignored her, climbing to the top bunk and getting under the covers. She desperately wanted to be alone.

'What's wrong?'

Maryam shrugged.

'You hardly said anything on the walk home.' Mum unwound the scarf from her head, climbed up the little ladder to Maryam's bed and sat on the edge. She looked at Maryam, her eyes saying 'just tell me'.

Maryam wasn't sure where to start. How could she explain that she always felt like other kids were making fun of her? That her parents' shop was a joke – it was nothing, something to steal from when you wanted. Why did no one else seem bothered that stealing was a crime? That it was just *wrong*? They would be bothered if it was from someone like them, but they didn't care that it was from someone like her.

'I don't know,' she said. 'I guess I feel sort of out of place at this school.'

'Why?'

She hesitated, trying to find the right words. 'It's like, they all seem to know each other already. And a lot of them aren't that nice.' She struggled with how else to describe it. What she didn't want to say to her mum was *they all seem richer than us*, but that was part of it – they called her part of town 'Grimsby', despite it being just half a mile away from the school. What she wanted to say even less was *I'm an outcast*. Instead, she said, 'I don't really want to talk about it.'

Mum rubbed her leg and sat there for a while. Then she said, 'I'm going to go cook some dinner. Don't worry. Everyone feels like this sometimes. But we love you, OK?'

Maryam nodded. 'I know.' She felt like she wanted to cry, from a combination of love and self-pity.

'The important thing is that we're all healthy,' said her mum. 'Don't let these sorts of things bother you.' She had been saying this lately – 'At least we're all healthy' – and Maryam knew it was because of the shop. She'd heard Mum on the phone to Dad on the way home, speaking in a hushed, stressed tone, thinking she and Hassan weren't listening. But they were – staying close, trying to hear not just Mum's voice, but Dad's on the other end. He spoke so loudly that it wasn't hard. He said rumour had it their landlord was going to raise the rent. The dry cleaner on the same block had his raised when his lease came up last month, but at least their parents had another year left.

Although Mum was stressed, she relentlessly focused on the positive. Maryam wanted to comfort her mum just then, rather than the other way around. But she climbed down and went to the kitchen, and Maryam could hear her heating oil in a pan and chopping onions, making an early dinner because she was working at the shop again tonight.

Lying in bed, Maryam remembered the rest of form

time that morning with a dull ache deep in her belly. Mr Whipple had announced an assignment, due before Christmas, to research their family trees. It was a project Maryam typically would have found interesting – she liked history. But then her heart sank with the next sentence: they were to work in pairs, and present each other's family history to the class. Mr Whipple had asked them to pair up on their tables. Incredibly lazy, thought Maryam. Why couldn't he at least *assign* pairs? Didn't he see how awkward this would be for her?

Leo and Ted had instantly paired up, and Maryam had looked up at Evie, with a small smile, to find her darting her eyes around the room, catching Arabella's, and rolling them. Maryam's smile had instantly fallen, and she looked down at her desk, humiliated, even as Evie had tried to recover. Evie had looked across the desk, and said, in a friendly tone, 'Partners, I guess?' But Maryam had felt unable to do anything other than nod, stifled by her shame. How silly she'd been to think that Evie wouldn't mind working with her.

Staring up at the ceiling, it occurred to Maryam how she must look to the others at school. Small and dark, with her school shoes from the supermarket and Hassan's old shirts. Even her glasses were wrong – she'd loved the purple colour when she'd got them last year, but now they looked childish. She rolled over. She didn't want to face the same kids in the same form room the next day. Why wasn't it enough to just work hard and keep to herself? Why did she *also* need to work with this person who obviously didn't want to work with her? She felt her eyes starting to burn again and climbed down, determined not to think about that morning any more.

'Hey, Mum?' she called to the kitchen, remembering the red folder from that morning.

'Yeah?' Mum asked over the sizzle of the frying onions.

'Could you look at this?' Maryam took the folder into the kitchen and approached the stove, holding out the top page with the nonsense writing on it. 'I found this folder in Nani's room, and look at this page. Do you know what it is?'

'Hmm.' Mum gave it a quick glance and turned back to the pan, tipping in the contents of a spice packet. The smell of frying cumin and turmeric filled the small kitchen, which was quickly getting steamy. She reached over to crack open the window. 'I don't know. You'll have to ask Nani.' She flipped the folder over and read the label. 'It says "Family Recipes" on the front,' she said, reading the Urdu. She then turned back to the single lined sheet, looking perplexed. 'Mari, why do you draw so many noses?'

Embarrassed, Maryam snapped the folder shut and retreated to her room. Family recipes? Although she couldn't understand the writing, it definitely looked like letters, not recipes. Walking back out of her room, she tapped softly on Nani's door, which was ajar.

'Yes?' the voice came from inside.

Maryam walked in to find Nani rolling up her prayer rug.

'S-sorry,' she stammered, backing out of the room.

'No, I'm finished,' Nani said. 'Come in.' She patted a spot on the shimmery gold bedspread, inviting Maryam to sit down next to her. Maryam sat with the folder on her lap and looked at the beige wall opposite her, where baby photos of Mum and Uncle Maz hung.

'What's this?' Nani asked, picking the folder up and holding it further from her face to read it.

'I don't know, actually,' Maryam said, 'that's what I was coming to ask you about. I found it in that box over there.' She gestured towards a broken cardboard box under the window. Taking the first page out of the folder, she handed it to Nani and said, 'Do you know what this writing is? It doesn't make any sense to me.'

Nani held it up, her gold bangles tinkling, and shook her head. 'The cover says "Family Recipes", but I don't understand this page at all.'

'Do you know where it would have come from?' Maryam asked.

'Well,' Nani said, 'it may have been my mother's. I have a lot of her things, but I don't always know what they are. I kept everything after she died.'

Maryam looked around the crowded bedroom – furniture, boxes and the bed took up all the space except a narrow path around the edge where tea-coloured carpet poked through.

'See, I was so young – only your age when she passed,' she said nonchalantly. 'I suppose it was my way of healing.'

Maryam gasped. Nani had never spoken about her parents, and Maryam couldn't believe she didn't know such a big thing as Nani's mum dying when she was still a child.

Nani waved her hand. 'Oh, it's OK. It's all a long time ago now.'

'How did she die?' Maryam asked.

'Tuberculosis,' Nani answered matter-of-factly. 'Life was hard in Pakistan at that time. Lots of illness, and lots of violence.' She went on, 'Anyways, I kept all these boxes of things. They helped me feel like a part of my mother was still with me. We had just moved from Delhi to Karachi, and her things were a little bit of home. I've had them for so long now I don't feel like I can throw them away.' She sighed.

Maryam was stunned that she'd never been told about any of this. *What violence? What illness?* But she stopped on something Nani had said that didn't make sense to her.

'Wait, you were born in Delhi? Isn't that India, not Pakistan?' Maryam asked, confused.

'Yes, but they used to be one country. Then when India was granted independence from Britain, it was also divided into two countries – India and Pakistan. All the Muslims like us travelled to Pakistan and everyone else went to India.'

Maryam had heard about this, vaguely. But Nani had always called herself Pakistani, never Indian. It was strange to think that she was born in India and had been Indian once.

'Was that good?' Maryam asked, hoping it wasn't a silly question.

'No.' Nani shook her head, and it was unlike her to give such a definite answer. 'It was terrible. Many people died.'

Maryam felt reluctant to ask any more questions of Nani, but didn't understand. If each religion had its own country, wasn't that fair? At the risk of asking a second silly question, she asked, 'Why?'

Nani turned the palms of her hands up as if she still didn't truly know the answer. 'The violence between Hindus and Muslims became very bad. Muslims in India were killed, as were Hindus in Pakistan. I will not tell you everything, because I have tried for most of my life to forget what I saw then.' She turned her hands back over and looked down at her wrinkled skin.

'But even without speaking of all the killings, lots of people had to leave their homes and start over with nothing. Like us. We went to Karachi and five of us lived in one room. We thought we would go back to Delhi one day, but then Amma died and we never did.'

Maryam looked at Nani in shock, as if this had happened yesterday, and not seventy years earlier. 'I'm sorry, Nani. I didn't know,' she said.

Nani rarely talked about her life in Pakistan, and when she did, it was funny titbits, like her brother skipping school to play cricket. Maryam thought back to how upset she'd been about school and she felt ridiculous.

As if reading her mind, Nani said, 'It's OK, Mari. Everyone's life is hard in a different way. We didn't have it so bad – we had what we needed. We were lucky.'

Nani considered the page again, brow furrowed, and turned it over to find the other side blank. 'I didn't understand most of what I kept from her,' she explained. 'See, Amma was the only one who could read and write English – an English friend had taught her. Someone whose father was in the British Army. I learned English later, but by then I'd forgotten about all of this stuff. I haven't gone through these things in years.'

She handed the page back to Maryam. 'I'm sorry, but I can't make any sense of it.'

Maryam tucked the page back in the folder. If her great-grandmother had learned to read and write English from a childhood friend, maybe these were nothing more than a children's game. She and Hassan used to try to make up languages. They'd never come close to anything that made sense, though.

Still, the handwriting looked like an adult's – narrow and flowing. Too serious to be a made-up language for fun.

4. Family Histories

Evie pulled her chair around to sit next to Maryam at their table, a big piece of paper in front of them. They were meant to be interviewing each other to learn as much as they could about their partner's family history. Evie drew a neat line down the middle with a ruler, and wrote *Maryam* on one side and *Evie* on the other.

Evie busied herself with this task to avoid making eye contact. She felt weird around Maryam who had sort of lost it with Ted, and then maybe caught her making a face at Bella. At break time, after Mr Whipple had announced the project, Bella had said, 'Well, *you* definitely didn't win the partner lottery.' Evie agreed.

But on the other hand, Maryam was clever, and always seemed to work really hard, so maybe they'd at least get a good mark on the project. As long as they didn't have to do an awkward presentation or performance together, it might be fine.

Mr Whipple made his way around each table, a notebook in his hand, as he ticked off who had done their homework – a family tree. Evie unfolded hers proudly: she'd made it look like an actual tree, with the branches and names written in bright marker, colour-coded by generation. She'd stayed patiently on the phone with her gran for an hour, who had given her far too much detail about her own father's military pursuits. She looked over at Maryam, who had lines and boxes drawn in blue pen on a sheet of lined paper in her book. The top of her tree had some blank spaces and question marks.

Across the table, Leo was unrolling a poster board with photos and typed labels pasted on.

'Keen much?' Ted quipped.

'My nanny did it for me,' Leo said with a laugh, and they both chuckled and fist-bumped.

Maryam turned away, closing her book.

'So,' Evie said, taking the cap off her marker and attempting to overcome their bad start, 'Shall I go first?'

Maryam nodded, looking down.

'OK, so . . .' Evie said, trying to think of a question. 'Where were your parents born?'

'Here,' Maryam said. 'London. They both grew up down the road, actually.'

'Really?' Evie said. 'That's crazy!'

'Is it?' Maryam asked.

'It's just that it seems like it used to be . . .' Evie paused – the word she wanted to say was 'rough', but she stopped herself, 'different around here.'

'Yeah, I guess,' Maryam said. 'They say there's, like, a lot more posh people than there used to be.'

Evie didn't know what to say to this. Did Maryam mean people like her were the posh people? She wasn't posh though, actually. Just . . . normal. She hadn't realised it before, but none of the parents of anyone she knew had grown up in their neighbourhood. At the front of the class, Mr Whipple was quietly writing a list of prompts on the whiteboard: who, what, when, where, why, how. Evie made a note in Maryam's column and moved along with her questions.

'What do your parents do?'

Maryam's face flushed red and she picked at her cuticles. 'They run a corner shop,' she said softly.

Evie thought back to last Wednesday and understood. So *that's* why she'd gotten so upset. Why hadn't Maryam just said so? It would have put Ted in his place. But she was probably embarrassed.

'I'm sorry about last week,' Evie said. Maryam instantly brightened, not with a smile, but with eyes that looked up at hers. 'Ted can be an idiot sometimes.' She glanced at Ted and Leo on the other side of the table, who had written nothing at all on their paper and were looking at a magazine hidden, not very subtly, under their books.

'Thanks,' Maryam said. Evie started to write *Parents run a corner shop*, but thought about how Maryam had been too embarrassed to admit it, and wrote *Parents in the food industry* instead. Maryam half-smiled.

'It's true, isn't it?' Evie said.

Mr Whipple announced that it was time to switch over. They hadn't got very far at all, but Maryam gripped her freshly-sharpened pencil and began.

'OK, so what do your parents do?'

'My mum works for a mental health charity,' Evie started.

'So she's a therapist?' Maryam asked.

'No, she's the director of communications.' Maryam frowned and wrote *Mum works for a charity.*

'My dad works for a start-up,' Evie continued. 'It's an app that lets you share bikes with other people in your neighbourhood.'

'So . . . he brings bikes to people?' Maryam asked.

'No, he works in an office. He does business development,' Evie said. Maryam blinked back at her. 'You can just write *works for a start-up.*'

'These jobs are complicated,' Maryam said, following Evie's instructions on what to write down.

'I guess,' Evie said. 'I don't really know what they do, to be honest.'

Mr Whipple came to their table and examined everyone's homework. 'Very nice, Evie,' he said, and Evie felt a small swell of pride that she tried not to show. He ticked Maryam's name off but didn't comment.

Maryam's eyes went to Evie's page, and Evie began to roll it up, not wanting to embarrass Maryam any further. But Maryam stopped her and pointed to a box at the top: *Katherine Hollins.* 'Who's this?' she asked.

'Oh, um, my gran's mother,' Evie said, not sure why Maryam was interested.

'Why was she born in India?' Maryam pointed to the line under her name, where *Born 1918, Delhi* was written.

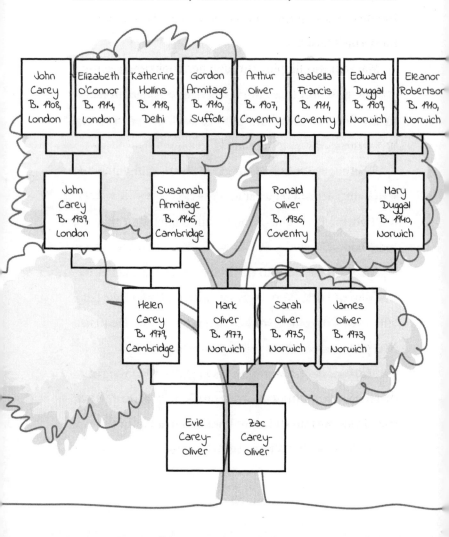

Evie herself had been surprised by this. 'It's random, right? My gran said that her mum's dad was an army officer in India.' Now that she tried to think of more details, she realised that Gran hadn't explained much about it – she'd quickly moved on to her father Gordon – Katherine's husband.

Maryam was flipping through her book now, seeming impatient to find something. Getting to her family tree, she pointed to *Safia Qureshi* towards the top of the page. In the box, she'd written *Born in Delhi, date unknown*.

A little sound of surprise escaped Evie's mouth. Their families had come from the same place? It seemed impossible.

'Wow,' Evie said. 'I wonder if they would have been there at the same time?'

'Maybe? I don't know when my great-grandmother was born, but she lived in Delhi until after she had children,' Maryam said. 'My grandmother – her daughter,' she pointed at a box that said *Shehenaz Bashar*, 'was born there. She said that her mum learned English from a friend who was the daughter of an English soldier.'

Maryam didn't seem to think this was notable,

39

but Evie's mind was racing ahead. What if her great-grandmother Katherine had been that friend? She knew that Gran's family had military connections, and that's why they were in India.

Was it possible that she and Wednesday were the descendants of women who actually knew each other in *India*? She checked herself – Delhi was a big place, and Maryam didn't even know when her great-grandmother was born. This might be a false lead, like often appeared in her mystery novels.

But if their families were actually connected, their final project was going to be unbeatable.

Maryam was working out a rough birthday for Safia based on her grandmother's birthday, and tutted as the lead snapped off her pencil. She pulled her backpack onto her lap to find a new one, and that's when Evie saw it: there, in the big unzipped pouch, a tattered, faded red folder.

It looked just like hers. Except, actually, the writing on the front looked different, although she couldn't see it clearly. Her mind was racing again with all the clues coming at her at once. Connected families, the same folder – maybe it all fit together.

Then she stopped herself. *You're being ridiculous,* she scolded with a firm voice inside her head. Surely, old red folders weren't so uncommon.

'What's that?' Evie asked in a casual voice, pointing at the folder, as Maryam began to lower her bag back to the floor.

Maryam drew in breath, as if she'd been caught doing something.

'It's nothing,' she said, zipping up the bag. 'Just an old folder I found in my grandmother's room.'

Her grandmother's room. Another strange connection. *Too strange,* Evie thought, *to not mean something.*

'Can I see it?' Evie asked. Maryam pursed her lips and looked down at the backpack. 'You know, unless it's personal or something.'

Maryam reluctantly brought the bag back up. 'No, it's not personal. It's just ...' She hesitated to finish her sentence. 'I found it a few days ago, but it's got some strange writing in it that doesn't make any sense.'

Evie clenched her jaw suddenly and felt the metal of her braces push back against her teeth. *Strange writing. Not a coincidence – there's something here.* She put her hand on Maryam's shoulder and felt Maryam draw back slightly. She realised she must look crazed.

'Wait, explain that bit – about the writing?' Evie said, trying not to sound too excited but looking at Maryam intently as she unzipped the bag. Evie hadn't really expected the folders to be connected to each other, but now it seemed like they must be. Maryam looked confused, and a bit flustered.

Evie tried to explain. 'It's just that I found one that looks like that in *my* grandmother's house, and it has strange writing in it too.' The defensiveness faded from Maryam's face. Evie eagerly took the folder out of Maryam's hands and her heart sank.

Not only was the writing on the cover not in English, it didn't even use the same letters as English. It wasn't the same writing as that in her letters after all. She'd jumped to conclusions too soon.

'It says "Family Recipes" in Urdu,' Maryam said in an offhand way.

Evie instantly rebounded from disappointment to excitement. *What on earth* . . . ? she thought. Evie stared hard at the label, not sure what she was looking for because

42

she didn't have the first idea how to read it. Without explaining any further, she got her own folder out of her bag and dropped it onto the desk. Seeing the *Family Recipes* label on the cover, Maryam's mouth snapped shut, her eyes went wide, and she looked at Evie. She opened her mouth to speak, but then closed it again.

They each rushed to take a sheet out of their folders and they put them side by side on the table in front of them, looking at the other's page. Both pages were old and a bit yellowed. The handwriting wasn't the same but it seemed to be in the same sort of language, and each looked like it was a letter to someone.

Evie felt a tingly chill go through her body. She had no idea what to make of it, and wasn't sure whether her thumping heart was from nerves or excitement. Her mind raced through explanations – could Maryam have seen her folder and decided to make a copy? No – there was no way she could have seen the pages inside. What if a sinister adult had made the folders to lure them into some kind of trap? But they would have had to get into both of their grandmothers' houses, which didn't seem probable.

'These *must* have something to do with our great-grandmothers, right?' Maryam asked.

Evie agreed that all of these facts must link together, but she couldn't make sense of how. Two great-grandmothers, at the same place and probably the same time. And two folders, found in their daughters' rooms, by their great-granddaughters, written in the same unintelligible language. It made her head spin.

Lost in thought, she hadn't noticed that the class had gone quiet in response to Mr Whipple standing and counting down with one hand in the air. She was suddenly conscious of how Ted and Leo were looking across the desk at her with curiosity, their eyes going to the matching red folders in front of her. She saw Ted trying to catch her eye, probably preparing to make a snarky face at her, but she pretended not to see and stashed the folder back in her bag.

The bell went, and Maryam said, 'We could look at them more at break?'

'Um,' Evie stalled. She imagined what would happen if she went off to a table with Maryam. Bella and Zoe would be instantly suspicious and would demand to know what was going on, and she wasn't ready to involve anyone else. She also wasn't too keen on explaining why she was suddenly hanging out with Wednesday. And yet, what she really wanted to do was spread out all the papers in their folders and figure out what in the world was going on. Instead, she'd be sitting on the wall, listening to Bella talk about other people and pretending to laugh at the boys' clownish behaviour.

'I need to do something else at break,' Evie said lamely, unable to think of a decent lie, 'but let's talk about it tomorrow in form time.' She quickly slung her bag on her shoulder, and skipped up to meet Bella, who was already walking out the door.

DELHI, INDIA

1929

5. Safia

Safia sighed. She reached into the paper bag of *chakri* that she'd just bought from the man over the road, the savoury rice sticks turning to paste in her mouth and leaving rice dust and grease on her fingers. The air felt thick and heavy, even in the shade under the canvas awning that stretched in front of her parents' fabric shop. Just as she looked out at the market-lined street in front of her and thought to herself that it needed to rain, one fat raindrop plopped on the awning, and then another. Her abbu came from the back to make sure the table was under cover. Safia backed up, careful not to touch any of the bolts of fabric with her greasy fingers – something she'd been told off for many times before.

Soon the skies opened up and the rain came down in

thick sheets, the dirt road turning to mud. People in the street quickened their pace and huddled for cover along the edges of the street. Two such people – an Indian woman and a white girl – came under their own awning for shelter. Safia looked down at her bag, avoiding eye contact.

Abbu called for Amma and when the Indian woman said hello Safia realised she'd seen her before. She recognised the green-and-white print of her sari as a fabric they had on one of the rolls somewhere on the table. Amma chatted to her about the price of things, and about the weather. The woman's name, she overheard, was Anjali.

Safia stole a glance up at the girl, whose light blue eyes she found to be staring straight back at her. The girl smiled and Safia snapped her head back down to her paper bag. She saw English people all the time, usually soldiers patrolling the street or civil servants hustling to their offices in linen suits, but she'd never actually interacted with one.

'Hello,' the girl said, undeterred by Safia's shyness. 'I'm Kathy.'

Safia ventured to raise her eyes. Kathy's freckled face dripped with rain and her orange-yellow hair frizzed like a halo around her head. She looked kind. Safia didn't speak English but she could work out Kathy's meaning.

'Hello,' she said, mirroring Kathy's words.

Then Kathy said something else that Safia couldn't understand, except for the word *ayah*. Safia understood that Anjali was Kathy's *ayah* – her nursemaid. But the single word floated in a sea of incomprehensible English. She furrowed her brow in confusion. Kathy seemed to understand that Safia couldn't speak English and pointed to herself. 'I'm Kathy.' Then, she pointed at Safia and said, 'You?'

Safia, catching on, said, 'Safia.' The girl smiled and said something else unintelligible, so Safia just smiled along. She chattered away happily, seeming not to mind that Safia couldn't follow. The rain was slowing to individual drops again, the storm easing as quickly as it had come on. Anjali turned to go.

'Goodbye, Safia,' the girl said. Then she said something else.

'Goodbye, Kathy,' Safia replied. The words felt heavy in her mouth, difficult to get out.

Then Kathy trailed Anjali back into the soggy road,

51

stepping on the edges of brown puddles rather than avoiding them, and soon getting mud on her white knee socks. She looked back at Safia and waved again.

Kathy came back the next day, this time on her own.

'Hi, Safia,' she said, approaching the table.

'Hi,' Safia replied, parroting her again. She could feel her amma's suspicious eyes glancing at her. Amma would be thinking that Kathy wasn't supposed to mix with Indians, that the girl's parents wouldn't approve.

'Safia,' Amma said. 'Take this and go buy some *tail*. Then go directly home.' She handed Safia a few rupees and a jar, and from her serious stare Safia knew that the errand was meant to send her and Kathy in different directions. Safia wasn't usually allowed to venture out alone, but Amma seemed to think it was worth it on this occasion.

Safia took the money in her hand and walked out from behind the table. She didn't know the word for goodbye so just said '*khuda hafiz*' to Kathy. But Kathy seemed not to get the hint, and didn't understand Urdu anyway, and followed her as she crossed the street. It was blazing hot and so bright it was hard to look directly at anything.

Safia didn't want to be rude to Kathy, but also didn't want to make Amma angry. So, she carried on, slowly enough that Kathy could keep up, but not looking directly at her. Eventually, Kathy paused and tapped Safia on the arm and then shrugged her shoulders and turned up her palms, as if to say *where are we going?*

Safia shielded her eyes with her hand and showed Kathy the money.

'Money,' Kathy said.

Safia then made a motion with her fingers that looked like walking. And pointed to one of the shops down the road.

'Ah, shopping,' Kathy guessed.

'Shopping,' Safia repeated slowly. Kathy pulled a small book and a charcoal pencil from her satchel and handed them to Safia. Safia wasn't sure what it was Kathy wanted her to do with these things, but she was good at drawing. So, she sketched a little map of the street and the shop and handed it back to Kathy.

'Nice sketch.' Kathy's face lit up. Then she said something else Safia couldn't make out.

They continued down the crowded street to Samir's shop, where Kathy followed Safia through the crowd. The stuffy shop smelled strongly of oils, spices and masalas – and of people. Kathy looked confused and captivated, her eyes darting all around, from the crowd of people to the scales on the counter and back again.

Safia thrust her arm up over the crowd, holding her money and her jar up, and Samir took it, looking surprised to see her alone. 'Yes, Safia?'

'Some *tail*, please,' Safia ordered, and Samir dipped a long ladle into a big tub of oil behind the counter, filled up Safia's jar and gave this to Safia along with her change.

The jar was actually quite heavy, and Kathy took it from Safia without asking. When they were back on the street, she held it up to Safia and instructed, 'This is oil.'

Then she pointed to Safia, who understood that Kathy wanted to know the words in Urdu.

'*Tail*,' she said, pointing to the jar. Kathy repeated this to herself, but the word didn't sound quite right to Safia's ears. She'd never heard an English person try to speak Urdu before.

Kathy giggled and Safia frowned back in confusion.

'Tail,' Kathy started, but Safia didn't understand what she said next and started laughing herself as Kathy turned around and wiggled her bottom. Only when Kathy took out her notebook, drew a cat, and then an arrow pointing at its rear, did she understand. Kathy wrote the word *tail* in English next to the drawing. Safia repeated the new word – *oil* – to herself as they walked home. Kathy heard this, wrote the word *oil* on her notepad below the cat and tore out the page, handing it to Safia. The letters were a complete nonsense to her. English words were all little circles and straight lines. She gestured for the pencil and wrote the sounds in Arabic letters so she could read them.

She wondered why Kathy was so intent on teaching her English. Or, for that matter, on being her friend. But she knew good luck when she saw it.

She came to the tall door on the side of her pink concrete building – the same one as her parents' shop – and walked up the staircase to her own flat on the first floor. Kathy named the objects the whole time – *This is a door, these are the stairs, this is your home* – until Safia started to get used to the little words – *this, the, is, a* – that were the most difficult. She made a quick sketch and a note for each noun as Kathy said it.

Inside her flat, her older brothers Abid and Ali squatted

on the floor and played marbles. They didn't look up, and Safia brought the jar through to the kitchen at the back of the house and sat it next to where her nani squatted over a low stove. She was stirring stew in an iron pot, humid and fragrant steam surrounding her.

'Thank you, Safia,' she said, turning her hunched back to greet her grand-daughter.

'Do you need anything, Nani?' Safia asked.

'No, child,' the old woman said.

Safia was conscious that Kathy hadn't followed her into the kitchen, and when she walked back out to the main room of the flat, she found Kathy watching Abid and Ali's game of marbles at a distance.

'Why have you brought this English girl home?' Ali asked Safia, without looking up, as she walked into the room. Safia bristled until she remembered that Kathy couldn't understand Urdu.

'I didn't bring her home. She just . . . followed me here,' Safia replied.

'Followed you here? Is she a stray cat?' Ali quipped, shooting his marble. He ran his hands through his hair as he missed.

'No, she's not. Her name is Kathy. Be nice.'

Kathy had been following this exchange like a dog watching a game of tennis, but stopped and brightened at the mention of her name.

'Yes, hello, I'm Kathy,' she said, looking at Ali, who blinked back, disarmed by her friendliness. Kathy turned to Safia, waiting to be introduced. She paused, trying to recall the right words.

'This ... is ... Abid,' she said in halting English, walking over to Abid, who seemed to shrink at the sound of his name. 'And ... this ... is ... Ali,' she said, staggering the words out, pointing towards Ali. Ali's jaw dropped.

'Since when do you speak English?' he said in disbelief.

'Since Kathy taught me,' Safia said proudly.

'Why doesn't she learn Urdu?' Ali replied challengingly. 'She lives in this country, after all. And if she's going to come to our home, she needs to take her shoes off.'

Safia snorted at her brother, knowing he was just refusing to show he was impressed. Kathy looked at Safia quizzically for an explanation.

'He say hello,' Safia mumbled. She began to point to the shoes still on Kathy's feet, when her nani shuffled into the room and darted at her, wide-eyed and panic-stricken.

'Safia!' she said, propelling herself forward on her walking stick. 'Who is this English girl? What are you doing bringing her into our home? Have you considered that her parents may not want her here?'

Safia did not attempt to answer any of these questions. She turned to Kathy reluctantly and made a face she hoped would be understood as 'I'm sorry'. She once again made the walking symbol with her fingers. Then, she said, 'Goodbye.'

Kathy nodded her understanding and, taking another look around the flat, smiled and said, 'Goodbye.'

When Kathy turned around, her grandmother was shaking her head, but met her eyes with a curious look before hobbling back to the kitchen.

'If you learn English, you'd better teach me, *behn*,' Ali said, smiling.

Safia wondered if she would, in fact, learn English. The thought filled her head with dreams.

6. Kathy

Kathy sat cross-legged in a narrow alleyway, her back against a stone wall, as she scratched out a sentence with chalk on her slate. Safia squatted next to her with her own slate, watching as she wrote. Her friend Naeem from her neighbourhood – a kind boy, broad around the middle with a dark complexion – sat on the other side of her, restlessly batting stones with a stick at the bright pink building opposite them.

The alleyway led onto a small but busy street, where oxen pulled carts full of supplies, men carried buckets of water hung on either side of a long pole, and street vendors called out to passersby. But no one paid them much notice in the alleyway. It felt like they could see without being seen. And Kathy needed to not be seen here, in Safia's neighbourhood in the old city, on her own.

Kathy had taken an extra slate from school that morning, slipping Ruth Turner's into her leather satchel when her back was turned. Ruth Turner was incredibly stuck-up, so Kathy didn't feel too bad about it.

Kathy put her chalk down, the sentence finished, and Safia carefully copied it: *The monkey ate a banana.*

Kathy had recently taken in a monkey she'd seen jumping around her garden. She'd asked Safia how to say 'monkey' in Urdu, and Safia had said 'bandar', so that became his name. Bandar showed Kathy why 'cheeky monkey' was a phrase, often stealing her hat or her food, or, most amusingly, chucking its poo at people walking by. Mother was quite annoyed at it, but not yet at Kathy, as she didn't realise that it lived mostly in Kathy's room.

Turning to Kathy, Safia said in halting English, 'The monkey ate a banana.'

It amazed Kathy that in just a few months of learning English, Safia could speak it. She felt a combination of pride in her teaching skill and jealousy that she had barely learned a word of Urdu. But Safia hadn't been nearly as interested in teaching her Urdu as she had in learning English, and to be fair, Kathy was just happy to have a friend. All the better if she could chat in her own language.

'That's right,' Kathy said. 'That's really good, Safia.'

'Thank you,' Safia said, looking down bashfully and skilfully drawing a monkey. 'Ali say it strange that I learn to read English but I cannot read Urdu.'

'Pardon?' Kathy turned and looked at Safia, who kept looking down, refusing to meet her gaze. She thought Safia must have mixed up her words. 'You can't read?'

It was inconceivable that she was illiterate. She was eleven years old, and as far as Kathy could tell, fantastically clever. It had taken her a mere few weeks to learn the English alphabet and begin working out words. But Safia just shook her head.

'Well, whyever not?' she asked, stunned.

Safia shrank away slightly. Naeem said something else in Urdu and Safia replied in a hurried, annoyed tone. She pursed her lips in frustration, and Kathy could tell that she didn't have the words to say what she was thinking in English.

'I . . . can read a bit,' Safia started defensively, then

paused. 'I know how to read the Quran, so I know the letters. But I do not know how to read properly.'

'But, surely your parents or your brothers could teach you,' Kathy argued.

Safia stood up from the ground, brushed the pebbles off the back of her *shalwar kameez*, and looked down to where Kathy sat. 'They are not so good at reading. Also, it is not proper for a girl.'

Kathy bit her bottom lip, not sure of what to say. 'Oh,' was all she could muster. She had misstepped. She saw that she knew so little about Safia and how different their lives were. It made her feel terrible for complaining about school.

'Please write me another,' Safia said matter-of-factly, sitting back down.

Kathy obliged. She wiped the writing and drawing away with her sleeve, took her chalk in her hand and began to write *The girl went to the shop.*

Then, the sounds of loud drums came from far off. Rhythmic thumping, getting closer.

It was getting louder, and beginning to sound more like music. Kathy recognised it as a procession for a Hindu festival. They were so different from her father's military parades. There would likely be scented smoke, and dancers, and a big wooden float on wheels. Sometimes Anjali would even dance in them, leaping and stomping, the bells on her ankles jangling. Kathy felt the music in her chest. It made her want to get up and move.

'Shall we go see it?' she asked. Kathy loved nothing more than a Hindu procession.

'No,' Safia replied without hesitation. Safia and Naeem exchanged a look.

'Why *not*?' Kathy whined. 'We can carry on with lessons later. Let's go see some dancing!'

'They are headed for the mosque,' Safia replied flatly.

Kathy didn't immediately understand the significance of this. Naeem started speaking angrily. Safia spoke to him in calm tones, but stood and looked down the street in the direction of the sound, her brow furrowed and the corners of her mouth turned down.

'What's wrong?' Kathy asked.

Safia once again worked to find the words. 'They . . . are Hindus. The mosque is Muslim. They are trying to . . . to . . .' She looked to Naeem, who of course was no help. 'To make it . . . difficult . . . to do the prayers.'

Kathy thought her worry was overblown. If it was a Hindu festival, then surely they could parade down the street? And the Muslims could still pray in their mosque?

'But it's just for one day,' Kathy said. 'And besides, I love the processions. Please, let's go and see if Anjali is in it!'

Safia flared her nostrils and then huffed out. Kathy realised that she'd misstepped again.

'The procession never goes by the mosque. This is new. They are . . .' She grew frustrated, slapping her hand against her thigh. 'They are . . .'

'Making a point?' Kathy tried, beginning to understand, but Safia didn't get the phrase. 'Um, doing it just to upset the Muslims?'

Safia nodded vigorously. 'Yes, yes. Making the point,' she said.

Then, they heard shouting mixed in with the drumming, which lost its rhythm. The procession wasn't getting closer any more. It had stopped, the drum banging not like music but like a battle cry, shouting voices drowning out the singing.

Then, men began to pour out of the mosque and into the street in front of them. They were angry, and soon they were a mob, stalling the procession. Safia watched them with horror in her eyes. She and Naeem kept glancing at each other, but neither seemed to know what to do.

Then Kathy saw Safia's brother, Ali, jog by. At fifteen, he was as tall as the others but much skinnier. She wondered if Safia had seen him too, until she heard her call out.

'Ali!'

Her cry was desperate. She ran after him into the throng of men, still holding the slate in her hand. The crowds parted for her, the men startled to see a girl amongst them, and she was able to grab her brother by the sleeve. He turned and spoke to her in Urdu but she wouldn't let go. He looked scared too. He looked like he didn't really want to go where the other men were going. Safia was pleading angrily. Naeem looked on, uncertain of what to do. Then, he sprinted off in the opposite direction.

In the meantime, Ali had managed to loosen his sleeve from Safia's grip, speaking to her reassuringly. He was surely saying something like 'it will be fine'. Then he was absorbed into the crowd.

Naeem came running up the street with a dark, pot-bellied man who could only have been his father. The man saw Safia and left Naeem with her, and then he himself waded into the street. Naeem said something in Urdu to Safia, who sniffed and followed Naeem's father with her eyes.

The crowd was getting denser, and had stopped moving. It was getting louder. All the men around them were yelling. The crowd had blocked the procession from moving forward, and the yelling had turned into fighting. All the while, the drum thumped.

'Ali . . .' Safia started explaining to Kathy, shouting to be heard. 'Naeem's father go to bring him back.' Her eyes searched the crowd. '*Pagal* Ali,' she muttered.

Kathy didn't understand, but had the feeling Ali had done something foolish. She could see Naeem's father jostling to get through the horde, and then lost sight of him. She began to look for a way out as men started crowding into the alleyway behind them, trapping them. She reached for Safia's hand and pulled gently at her wrist, but Safia didn't budge. Her decision made, Kathy planted her feet to the ground and squeezed Safia's hand. Safia squeezed back weakly.

Kathy heard the clip-clopping of men on horses before Safia did. She knew they had come from the barracks in the Red Fort, and that if she could hear them, they were just around the corner. Kathy knew these riots happened sometimes, and that sometimes soldiers were wounded, carried back through the gates on a stretcher. Her father would often be on the scene – he used to be an officer in the Indian Army, but now he was a political officer, meaning, from what she could tell, that he tried to understand who was fighting with whom, and who would be fighting each other next. She'd never had any idea what the fighting was about, let alone seen a riot up close. She wondered what her father would do if he knew she was here.

But the thought was interrupted by Naeem's father coming back towards them, half-carrying a limping Ali with a bloody nose. Drops of blood dotted his white *kurta*. He cast his eyes down, looking sorry for himself. Naeem's father was scolding him. Safia marched up to them and pulled Ali into a hug. She cried, looking more like a young child than she usually did. Ali hugged her back. Naeem stepped forward and gently took the slate that Safia still held in her hand, and passed it to Kathy.

Kathy accepted the slate and took this as her cue to go. She extended an arm to give Safia a pat on the back goodbye, but before she could she heard a man's voice behind her.

'Miss Hollins!'

Kathy turned around with a gasp. Anyone who called her Miss Hollins was British, and anyone British would be appalled to see her here.

Marching towards her were two figures in tan army uniforms and knee-high boots, with rifles slung round their bodies with a leather strap. As they got closer she could see under their helmets that they were Lewis and Birdwood, two of the young officers in her father's regiment. Without a further word, Lewis swept her up, carried her swiftly away from the crowd, and put her on his horse, Birdwood staying close and pointing his rifle at everyone around them. Kathy's chest tightened as she thought of the trouble she'd be in. She knew she'd been in a dangerous situation, but also knew the bigger problem would be that she was socialising with Indians unsupervised. Birdwood mounted his own horse and they rode up backstreets, avoiding the crowds. Neither of them said anything until they were back in her neighbourhood of Civil Lines, nearly at her house.

At last, Lewis pulled on the reins, and they stopped in front of Kathy's house. Lewis helped her dismount and said, 'Miss, how did you come to find yourself at the scene of a riot? It was entirely unsafe for you to be there.'

'*Entirely* unsafe,' echoed Birdwood from up on his horse.

Kathy searched for a lie. 'I just . . . went for a walk, and then I got lost.' The officers looked sceptical. 'I'm ever so grateful you found me and rescued me. I can't thank you enough.'

This seemed to soften them somewhat, and she hoped it was enough to stop them from telling her parents.

As if reading her mind, Birdwood said, 'Of course, you understand that we'll need to inform your parents of this.'

Kathy's stomach dropped but she tried not to show it on her face. 'Of course,' she replied. Birdwood had always been a snivelling bootlicker. When he turned his back, she stuck her tongue out. Lewis saw her and raised an eyebrow, but said nothing.

*

Her father was late for dinner that night. The shutters were closed to keep the room cool, and Anjali lit the candelabra with a long match. Kathy's mother sat at one end of the table, opposite her father's empty place. Her blonde hair looked silver in the candlelight, her diamond necklace glinting. Her glittering appearance stood in strange contrast with her sour expression.

They sat in silence and eventually her mother called for Pooja, the cook, to bring the food in – chicken stewed in a dark red gravy. Kathy's mother spread her napkin on her lap and began daintily cutting her chicken, scraping the sauce off it with a look of disgust.

Kathy sat, chewing her food and finding the warmth of the spices and the sweetness of the sultanas delicious. She wished she could sop up the gravy with a piece of *roti* as she saw Pooja and Anjali doing when they ate, but mother would never allow that. She already said that Kathy was developing the poor table manners of a native.

Kathy felt conscious of the sound of her own chewing as she waited for her mother to say if she'd received a visit from Lewis and Birdwood. She cleared her throat and Kathy knew it was coming.

'Katherine,' she began. It was never good when she started with 'Katherine'. 'I've received some most distressing news from two young officers today.' As she said this, she looked not at Kathy, but at the chicken she was cutting. 'They said they found you near a riot, amongst a group of Indians.' At this last part, she looked Kathy in the face.

'Yes,' Kathy said. She decided that she'd stick with the same line she'd used before. 'I went for a walk, and I got lost.'

Her mother raised her chin slightly and looked down her nose at her, as if appraising whether she was lying.

'That was an extremely dangerous situation you got yourself into, not to mention one unfit for a young lady of your stature.'

Kathy was not surprised to hear this, as Mother had recently begun noting the many things she did that were 'unfit for a young lady of her stature'. These included having dirty fingernails, eating in public, climbing trees, and continuing to wear her favourite dress even though it had got a bit short lately. When combined with climbing trees, the short dress especially irked her mother.

But she stayed silent, as she could tell her mother had more to say.

'You are no longer a child, Katherine. You must begin to understand that. These people are not like us. They are not *civilised*.'

Kathy wasn't sure she knew what her mother meant. Why did being eleven and not seven have any bearing on who she should spend time with? In fact, she wasn't even sure what her mother meant by 'civilised'. But she just said, 'Yes, Mother.'

'I will speak to Anjali about accompanying you whenever you leave the barracks. You are not to go roaming about on your own any longer. Am I understood?'

'Yes, Mother,' Kathy said again. She hoped she hadn't gotten Anjali in trouble, but suspected she had.

She wondered what she'd be able to get away with now. There was, surely, a way to keep seeing Safia – she just needed to figure it out.

In her room, Kathy took a piece of writing paper from her desk and the pen from the inkwell and sat down to write a letter.

Dear Safia,

I hope Ali is not hurt too badly. I'm sorry, but I will not be able to meet for a little while. I will come see you as soon as I can. Until then, understanding this letter will be your lesson. Your homework is to memorise the conjugation of the verb 'to go'.

Your friend,

Kathy

Kathy knew that the letter would be too difficult for Safia to read, but hoped she would use the dictionary she'd brought her. She turned the letter over and wrote the conjugation of 'to go' in every tense, which she herself actually found quite challenging.

She folded up the letter and wondered when she'd be able to take it to Safia. There was shuffling in the corridor, and Kathy heard the sweep of Anjali's broom making its way down the hallway. She popped her head out the door. Anjali was sweeping ferociously, like the bamboo floor was her mortal enemy. Kathy looked on silently.

Anjali's eyes were furious and she muttered to herself in Hindi. There were a few English words that Kathy picked up, like 'uncivilised' and 'English', which she spat out like a pistachio shell. Kathy didn't know what to do with this mood that she'd never seen in Anjali before.

She cleared her throat. 'Anjali,' she began.

Anjali startled. She clearly hadn't seen Kathy there, and her eyes went from angry to frightened.

'Don't worry, please,' Kathy said. 'You have a right to be angry. I'm sorry about what Mother said.' Then, realising Anjali had been home all afternoon, she asked, 'Did you not go to the procession? Did you hear what happened?'

Anjali's face clouded with anger again, and she resumed working her broom, stabbing at the corners as if hunting something. 'No, Miss Kathy, I did not go. And yes, I did hear. I knew they were going to parade in front of the mosque and I wanted no part of it. And look at what has happened now.'

She swept and carried on talking, and it seemed to Kathy that Anjali was mostly talking to herself. 'These men, these idiot men and their pride will be the end of us all.'

Kathy wanted to stop her and ask what she meant. But Anjali was sweeping as if the broom was a weapon, and carried on, her voice growing wobbly with emotion. 'And now the fighting will continue tonight. Each time it gets worse. These men, they think the war is with each other, their neighbours. Ha! The war is not between us. We'll simply tear ourselves apart.'

Kathy didn't understand what she meant when she said war, or who it was actually with. She wondered if the fighting would carry on in Kashmiri Gate, where Safia and Anjali both lived. She wondered if anyone Safia knew would be amongst the people fighting. But she hesitated to stop Anjali for an explanation when she was angrier than Kathy had ever seen her.

Anjali looked at Kathy, remembered herself, and a slightly panicked expression once again came over her face. She composed her voice. 'I'm sorry, Miss Kathy. It is not talk for children. Is there something you need?'

Kathy nearly told Anjali that she was meant to be a young woman now, no longer a child, but she thought better of it. And then she remembered why she had come out of her room.

'Um, yes,' Kathy said, reaching for the letter in her pocket. 'If you go to the market tomorrow, could you please take this to Safia? Her mother is the one who has the fabric shop.'

Anjali looked at the letter as if it was dangerous. She didn't take it.

'It says I'm going to stay away for a while,' Kathy said, hoping this would reassure Anjali.

Anjali nodded, took the letter, and tucked it into the folds of her sari.

LONDON, UK

PRESENT DAY

7. The Hiss

It was the kind of grey November day that spat at you on and off, and Maryam sat on a damp log on the side of the football pitch, where Hassan's class was finishing up their PE lesson. Maryam let her gaze wander over to the low brick wall, where a pack of kids from her form sat. Everyone was listening to Ted, and she imagined, with a burning in her chest, that he was retelling the story from last week and making her sound painfully awkward. Leo, and maybe Evie, would be backing him up. *Yeah, she was like an angry little gnome*, they'd say, *until she started crying.*

This was a game Maryam played sometimes – imagining the mean things others were saying about her. She knew it wasn't helpful, but she couldn't stop herself.

Maryam saw that Hassan was finished with PE and she waved him over. Hassan reluctantly jogged across the pitch, the hood of his sweatshirt pulled up. His friend Lennox sauntered behind him.

'Hey, there's something I need to show you,' Maryam said.

'Not now,' he said, looking across to the canteen. 'I'm starving.'

'Just give me thirty seconds.' Maryam took out the folder. 'Please.'

Hassan raised his eyebrows and set the timer on his watch. 'You got thirty seconds.'

Maryam rolled her eyes and took a deep breath. Then, speaking as fast as she could, she said, 'That folder I found in Nani's room? With the nonsense writing in it? It turns out it says "Family Recipes" in Urdu on the outside, but they aren't recipes, and they're *not* Russian either.' She handed Hassan the page and took another breath. 'I asked Nani and she doesn't have any idea what it is, but she said it probably came from *her* mother's things in Pakistan. But that's not even the crazy part.'

Hassan's timer went off. Lennox, who was still

standing at a distance, moaned, 'Come *on*. The queue is getting *massive*.'

'Lenno, go ahead and get me a cookie. I'll pay you back.'

'Bruh, stop lying. You never pay me back. But I'll get you your cookie.' He walked off with a bounce.

Hassan turned back to Maryam, nodding for her to go on.

'The crazy part,' Maryam said, 'is that there's this girl named Evie in my form, and she found a folder *just like it* in her grandmother's house. The cover is in English and not Urdu, but it *also* says "Family Recipes" and *also* has letters written in a nonsense language *just like these*.'

Maryam, having finished her speech, looked at Hassan as he studied the paper. He then took the folder and looked at the other loose pages in the pockets.

'This is mad, man,' he said.

'I know,' she said, 'and stop calling me man.'

'Who is this Evie girl anyway?' Hassan asked.

Maryam looked across the pitch to Evie and her friends, sitting on the wall. She thought with a pang about how Evie had said she needed to do something else at break – she sat laughing, looking up at a boy in mock horror who was standing on the wall on one leg and doing a sort of yoga pose. She didn't look like she'd needed to do anything at all.

Maryam gestured towards the group. 'Over there, with those girls on the wall. She's the one with the wavy blonde hair.'

Hassan squinted. He needed glasses but refused to wear them. 'What's she like?'

Maryam shrugged. 'She's OK, I guess. Some of her friends are pretty awful though.'

'Yo, maybe we should call the police,' he said, looking anxious.

'The police? What are they going to do about it?'

'I dunno, but what if it's, like, a trick someone is playing on you?' Hassan asked. 'It would teach them a lesson if the police came round their house.'

This had been Maryam's secret fear, and she felt slightly nauseous at the realisation that her big brother also thought she was someone who people might play a trick on.

Hassan saw her face and changed direction. 'Who

knows where this came from. Could be some creepy fifty-year-old dude who planted it. We don't know.'

Maryam considered this. It seemed highly unlikely.

'But the police might take it away,' she said. 'Let's just keep it to ourselves for the rest of the week. Deal?'

Hassan looked unsure, but Maryam heard his stomach growl and he looked over at Lennox in the snack line.

'Deal,' he answered reluctantly. 'I'll see what I can find on Lenno's phone,' he said, writing *Uvri Jrwzr* on his hand.

'OK. Just don't tell Lennox about it,' she pleaded.

But Hassan was already off. Maryam headed into the building the minute the bell rang, to top-set maths with Ms McVey. Ms McVey was a small, pale woman with a short, sensible haircut, who didn't try overly hard to make friends with the students, maybe because it was a subject that so many children hated.

She herself rather enjoyed maths – the summer she turned seven, her dad had written out all of the times tables on a big sheet of paper on her wall. He said that times tables were the most important thing she'd ever learn, and he'd get her a big cake – any cake she wanted – if she learned them all. She did, and true to his word, he'd taken Maryam to the supermarket and let her choose from a whole aisle of cupcakes, cakes with roses piped on top, and cakes shaped like animals. She chose the biggest one – a vanilla birthday cake with sprinkles on it that said it fed sixteen people. She had taken it home and eaten half of it for dinner before feeling extremely ill.

But her dad had been right in that all of the maths in school had been easy after that. Times tables, but also division and fractions, and now equations, seemed to come easier to her than to other kids. So it didn't scare her as much as the others when she walked in to find the words *Pop Quiz* on the board and Ms McVey handing out sheets of paper face down.

Maryam sat next to Arabella at her table, who seemed to scare everyone around her. Maryam was no different. Arabella was usually surrounded by a group of girls – including Evie, Maryam remembered at that moment – and almost always seemed to be demonstrating her superiority over someone else. She wasn't particularly clever or funny, but people seemed to respect her because her mum – Ms Underhill – was deputy head of the school.

When the sheet was placed in front of Arabella,

she pressed down the paper against the desk, trying to see through to the questions on the other side and save herself precious half seconds. When Ms McVey looked at her watch and said 'Go!' Maryam worked methodically through the questions, knowing she'd finish with plenty of time. She saw Arabella's eyes wandering over towards her paper and cupped her hand around the sheet to block her view. Arabella shifted a bit, leaning her body in Maryam's direction and looking down her little ski-slope nose, and Maryam turned her back towards her, irritated. When she glanced up, she saw Arabella staring her straight in the face. Her green eyes flashed with anger.

It was because Arabella expected to get what she wanted, and because she almost always seemed to, that Maryam decided that she wasn't going to back down. Arabella looked her in the eyes, annoyed that she wasn't being given access to Maryam's paper, as if she were *entitled* to cheat.

Maryam returned her glare, flared her nostrils, and hissed.

Maryam instantly wished she could suck the hiss right back into her mouth. She couldn't quite believe she'd done it, and knew instantly it was a mistake. Arabella's hand shot up immediately and she squirmed in her chair, sighing loudly. Maryam decided to quickly finish her quiz.

When Ms McVey finally noticed Arabella's theatrics, she came over and said, 'What is it, Arabella?'

'Maryam is making aggressive noises at me. It's making it impossible for me to concentrate.'

'That's only because she was trying to cheat,' Maryam muttered, feeling, without looking up, the eyes of the rest of the class move to her.

Ms McVey looked anxiously from Maryam to Arabella and back again, glanced at her watch, and called out, 'OK, pencils down!' to the rest of the class. There was the sound of pencils dropping, and when Maryam cast her gaze around the class, she saw them all craning their necks to get a view of what was happening. All except for Evie, who seemed to make a point of not looking in her direction.

Ms McVey looked worried. 'OK, let's just take this outside and talk it out.'

Ms McVey quickly collected the quizzes and led Maryam and Arabella over to a small table in the corridor.

Arabella started talking without being asked. 'She

thinks she's better than everyone just because she knows all the answers. Honestly, it makes me feel like I can't take part. And isn't that the motto of our school? "Everyone is welcome"?' Arabella had worked herself close to tears, her freckled face growing crimson.

'So let's talk about the facts of what happened. Maryam, why don't you start?'

'Well, we were doing the quiz, and I saw Arabella looking at my paper, so I put my hand around it. But then she just stared at me, like she was trying to *make* me show her my answers.'

'That's *not true*!' Arabella protested. Tears were now streaming down her face.

Maryam continued as if Arabella hadn't interrupted her. 'So . . . I hissed.'

'You . . . hissed?' Ms McVey asked, confused.

'Yeah. Look, I don't know why I did it. I'm sorry,' Maryam said, resigned to the fact that she would eventually need to apologise.

'I was looking *up*. That's how I *think*,' Arabella went on, undeterred. 'You know, my mother always says that different learners learn in different ways.'

'That's true,' Ms McVey said, wincing at Arabella's mention of her mother. 'And making strange noises isn't the way we express our feelings, Maryam.'

Maryam wasn't surprised when Ms McVey apologetically told her that she'd have a lunchtime detention in her classroom because she 'wasn't living the St Mary's values'. However, she also said to Arabella that she'd get a separate seat for quizzes in the future so she could 'look around' whilst thinking. It was a victory, of sorts.

At lunch, Maryam headed back to the maths classroom. Through the window to the courtyard, she could see Arabella dramatically telling a story – probably about her – to Evie and their other friend Zoe. Ms McVey handed Maryam a rag and a spray bottle that smelled like lemon chemicals and she began cleaning the desks. But actually, Maryam wasn't too upset about spending lunch break in the classroom.

'So, Maryam, how are you finding school?' Ms McVey was pretending to mark books, but she clearly wanted to have a conversation.

'OK.' Maryam wasn't sure how to respond. 'I do

actually enjoy art, and maths as well,' she said, then added, 'I'm not just saying that.'

'I'm glad to hear that,' Ms McVey said with a smile. 'And what about friends? Who do you like to spend time with?'

'Um . . . I'm actually OK on my own.' She scrubbed at a pen mark on the table. This didn't feel true, but Maryam thought it made her sound well-adjusted.

'It's good to feel comfortable on your own. That will serve you well in life.' There seemed to be something the teacher was trying to get at. 'But you'll need friends too.'

Maryam scraped at the pen mark with her fingernail, avoiding eye contact with Ms McVey. It wasn't that she didn't *want* friends – it was that she didn't know *how* to get herself out of this friendless state. It seemed like half the class already knew each other from the day they'd started secondary school and she knew no one. She'd had two good friends in primary school – Leah and Sumayya – but they both went to Willowfield now, like almost everyone else in their class, and she knew they were part of a chapter of her life that had finished. They'd sent texts to each other through their parents at the start of the school year, but she hadn't texted them in weeks. Now it was most of the way through autumn term, and she'd do anything to feel like there was someone on her side, or failing that, to make herself invisible.

'You also need to pick your battles,' Ms McVey said. 'Arabella might not be the best person to get into a fight with.' Maryam knew Ms McVey was right. Arabella would hold a grudge, and that would be far worse than cleaning duty.

Ms McVey got up to open the door for the next class to come in and Maryam slung her bag on her shoulder. She looked out the window and caught Evie's eye. Evie gave her a barely perceptible smile and then looked away. She tried to put out of her mind what Arabella would have been saying about her, avoiding the temptation to imagine how Evie might have joined in to mock her, might have told them all about the folders for story value, might even have made the whole thing up as a prank.

8. My New Friend Sarah

Evie and Zoe walked out of the school gates together, arms linked so they wouldn't lose each other in the mob of people trying to squish through the door.

Evie scanned the curb for her dad, who was picking her up for tutoring with Mrs Bernard – the low point of her week. Time went remarkably slowly in Mrs Bernard's dining room. It was like walking into some kind of vortex where every minute actually took five minutes to pass. Evie tried to delay this as much as possible, and she strode slowly towards the street.

'Gotta go. I've got swimming.' Zoe rolled her eyes.

'Tutoring,' Evie countered, deadpan.

'You win,' Zoe said with a laugh.

Evie heard someone behind her call her name. It was

Maryam, jogging to catch up with her and looking dishevelled with one sock dropping down. As if Maryam could suddenly sense this, she pulled her sock up and smoothed the stray bits of hair behind her ears. Evie pretended not to hear or see her in the crowd of people, and waved goodbye to Zoe, who was looking over her shoulder for where the voice was coming from.

Evie lingered by the fence, letting Maryam approach. Two older boys trailed behind her – one skinny, with baggy trousers and his tie done up too short, and the other tall and wide, wearing a big puffy coat.

'Hey,' Evie said to Maryam, casting a nervous glance at the two boys, who stopped a couple of metres away. The bigger one dipped his hand into a tube of barbecue crisps as he laughed to the smaller one. The smaller one, however, looked in her direction with a serious expression.

'Hi,' Maryam said, looking back at the boys.

'Who are they?' Evie asked, trying to sound casual.

'Oh, that's my brother Hassan and his friend Lennox,' she said. Evie now realised that they were obviously related, and felt silly for asking. 'Hassan searched some stuff on Lennox's phone and thinks the writing might be some sort of code.'

Her chest tightened at the thought of these random teenage boys knowing something about her. 'Oh, so you told them about this?' Evie hadn't told a soul, except Zoe.

'Yeah, but don't worry. They won't tell anyone else,' Maryam said. 'I was wondering if you wanted to have a closer look at the pages now?'

Maryam seemed too flippant about this. Surely they couldn't just start telling people.

'I haven't told anyone else,' Evie said, deciding that Zoe didn't count, 'and I wasn't planning to yet.' Maryam needed to understand that she couldn't just go around telling whoever she wanted, especially random Year Tens. She had no idea who these boys were. For all she knew, they could be spreading rumours about her on the internet. 'And I can't meet now – I have . . .' She stumbled on the word 'tutoring', feeling embarrassed that Maryam was so good at maths, but her own parents needed to spend loads of money on a tutor. '. . . an appointment. But I do have a phone.'

Maryam looked at Evie with wide eyes. 'You . . . have a phone. Cool. And it, like, goes on the internet?'

'Um, yes,' Evie said, awkward at how surprised Maryam seemed, and at the cluelessness of her question.

Out of the corner of her eye, she saw Bella come out of the school building. She'd spent all of lunch listening to Bella's emotional retelling of what had happened in maths, and her insistence that Maryam had 'behavioural problems'. Evie hadn't seen what happened, but she had seen Bella trying to cheat before. She also knew Bella was usually at her most dramatic when she was in the wrong. It would set her off to see Evie chatting with Maryam.

'Anyhow, I should go,' Evie said quickly, looking over to see that Bella had stopped to take her water bottle out of her bag. She was desperate to end the conversation before Bella got any closer. 'Maybe we could meet this weekend?' Even as she said it, Evie wasn't sure this was a wise suggestion.

'OK,' Maryam answered quickly, and looked at Evie as if waiting for her to suggest a plan.

But Evie needed to think. 'I'll see you in form time tomorrow,' she said. 'Bye.' She walked quickly to the school gate, took out her phone and pretended to text as a signal that the conversation was over.

'Eves!' Evie heard Bella calling across the courtyard, using a nickname that Evie quite liked. Despite this, her heart sank a bit that her plan to get away unseen had failed. Bella was jogging to catch her up.

'Hey,' she said. 'I've got half an hour until my mum finishes – want to hang out?'

'I wish,' Evie said honestly. 'I've got maths tutoring.' She mock-vomited.

'Well, maybe you'll become a maths genius like Wednesday,' Bella said. 'Hey, why were you just talking to her?'

Here it was – the part Evie had been trying to avoid. *Of course* Bella had seen her – she had only been a few metres away.

'I was just asking her a question about the maths homework,' Evie lied quickly, pleased with herself.

'Why didn't you just ask me? My mum *is* a maths teacher,' Bella said with an annoyed note in her voice. Her steps got slightly stompier. 'I should probably change her nickname to Mog after she hissed at me.'

'Mogyam,' Evie muttered absent-mindedly. She was so used to batting around puns with Bella that she didn't think to stop herself. Her chest burned with dread as she realised a mean new nickname may have been born.

'Mogyam!' Bella giggled hysterically. 'That's so good. Oh, I'm going to use that.'

Please don't, Evie thought to herself.

Just then Ted and Leo sauntered up, smirking as usual. 'Hey, Underhill,' Ted said to Bella. 'Heard you got caught cheating.'

Bella's eyes narrowed and her freckled face flushed. 'I *wasn't* cheating,' she said with venom. 'It was that loser Wednesday. She needs help.'

Please don't tell them about Mogyam, Evie pleaded internally.

'Yeah,' Leo said. 'She totally melted down in form last week. Evie was there.' He looked at Evie for affirmation.

Evie wondered if she should tell Leo that Maryam's parents owned a shop like the one Ted had shoplifted from. But then again, maybe that would just give them more ammunition. Evie stood lamely, eventually nodding half-heartedly.

'*See?*' Bella screeched at Ted, as if Leo's opinion was scientific fact. 'Honestly we should teach her a lesson.'

Please don't tell them about Mogyam.

'We came up with a good name for her,' Bella said, raising her eyebrows with a sly grin.

Oh God, Evie thought, *here it comes.*

'*Mog*yam. Get it? Cuz of the hiss?' She looked from Leo to Ted as if she deserved credit. 'Except cats are meant to have good vision, aren't they?'

Evie felt irritation at Bella spreading like a rash across her skin. She wanted to claim the praise that was rightfully hers. She also wanted to run away. The conflict paralysed her yet again, and she just stood there. It occurred to her that cat's-eye glasses might somehow play into the banter, but she kept her mouth shut.

Out of the corner of her eye, she spotted her dad's car, quickly said goodbye, and felt utterly useless as she got in. She couldn't shake the guilty niggle that she should have defended Maryam. But it probably wouldn't have even made a difference.

She found Dad on his phone and climbed into the back seat.

'How was school?' he asked.

Evie shrugged. 'Fine, I guess.' Evie's mind stayed

on Bella. Why did she even care if Bella was mean to Maryam? She didn't really. It was more that she always did this – got obsessed with turning everyone against a person she'd decided was evil, or weird, or her competition. She'd done it to that girl Hilda in primary school who'd eventually transferred out, and now she was doing it again.

Then, with dread, she remembered her panicked suggestion that she meet up with Maryam over the weekend. Maybe she should backtrack, make an excuse. Then again, she did want to have a better look at the contents of Maryam's folder. She'd hardly had time to inspect it the other day, or to even process the weirdness of the fact that Maryam had found a nearly identical folder with equally unintelligible letters in it. She thought back to what Maryam's brother had told her – that it might be a code – and wondered if it could be true. But what was so secret that her great-grandmother needed to communicate in code? It seemed like it must mean something that the letters were written during the Second World War, but what could her great-grandmother, a maths teacher, have to do with that? Evie had the feeling she was onto a mystery that needed solving. She'd never been great at puzzles, and was actually happy that there was someone to help her solve this one.

She'd keep the plan, she decided. But not at her house – there was always a chance that someone would drop by. She would ask if she could go to Maryam's to work on the class project.

'Hey, Dad,' she called up to the front seat, 'can I go to a new friend's house this weekend?'

But then someone called his phone, which came through the car speaker. Dad cursed under his breath.

'Um, sure,' he said, breathing out hard before taking the call and answering in a professional-sounding voice, 'This is Mark.'

He spoke in accommodating tones to a peeved-sounding woman on the other end. Evie took out her phone and checked her messages. She felt her stomach swell into her throat as she opened a group chat with half their form in it. There were twelve messages, the first from Bella:

Evie thought of the best nickname after that hissing incident: Mogyam!

She then posted a picture of a cartoon cat, which she'd drawn plaits on. Then, a series of people posting laughing emojis, laugh-crying emojis, and *LOL*. Leo posted *Nice one, Evie*. Evie's stomach turned to think she was getting praise from Leo. It was just like Bella to drag her into something mean. But she couldn't undo it now. She decided the best thing she could do was nothing, and put the phone back in her bag.

Tutoring always left Evie feeling like a deflated balloon, and she slumped limply through the door when they returned home. She heard Zac hopping down the steps, and he flung open the door, his arms and legs in starfish position, and yelled, 'Yeahhhhhhhh!'

She could tell from this reaction, even before entering the kitchen and smelling the baked cheese smell, that they were having lasagne for dinner. Zac bounced around the kitchen island, singing 'yum, yum, yum, yum' to himself.

They sat down, and Mum carried over a large casserole dish, set it on the table and cracked the brown, bubbly top with a spoon, making a crunching sound, before scooping into the cheesy middle. The four of them all dug in, and at first the only sound was of forks and knives sawing away at the hardened cheese, then scraping up bites from plates. Evie's mum broke the silence.

'So, Kate just messaged saying that Bella's been having a really hard time at school. Says she's being bullied by another girl.' Bella really hadn't wasted any time telling her version of the story to her mum. Evie looked down at her plate, focusing intensely on her lasagne and saying nothing. 'Do you know anything about that?'

'No. She got into an argument with this girl, but I wouldn't say she was being bullied,' Evie said. She wondered if she should do more to defend Maryam, but left it there.

'Kate said the girl, what was her name . . .' She closed her eyes, trying to remember it. 'Maryam! Maryam was very aggressive towards Bella, and also has been displaying some pretty strange behaviour.'

'The school really needs to be nipping that sort of thing in the bud,' Dad added between mouthfuls.

Evie felt her face getting hot and could tell she was turning red. She knew she should just stay quiet, but she couldn't hold back her annoyance.

'Bella's exaggerating,' she blurted out. 'Maryam didn't do anything that bad.' Her mum raised her eyebrows.

'Honey, are you sure?' Mum asked. 'Kate seemed to feel really strongly about it.'

'Well, I'm sure Bella made herself sound like the world's biggest victim,' she said. She wiped her palms, which were suddenly feeling sweaty, on her legs.

'Evie?' Mum looked at her seriously. 'Is everything OK with your friends?'

'Yeah, everything's fine,' Evie said quietly, wondering if this was true. She knew she sounded like she was getting worked up. She ran her tongue along her braces and tried to sound more reasonable. 'I just think Bella is being unfair, that's all.'

'Well, I suppose we don't know what some children have been through. Sometimes the ones with the worst behaviour have had horrific home lives,' Mum said.

Evie furrowed her brow and squinted her eyes in frustration. She opened her mouth to come back that Maryam wasn't actually badly behaved, but stopped herself.

Mum was looking at her tenderly. 'I'm glad you stand

up for what you think is right,' she said. 'It just sounds like you might be having some tension with Bella.'

Evie wanted to take this invitation to talk about it, but she wasn't sure what she was feeling. It wasn't like she was *fighting* with Bella. And she actually still really liked hanging out with Bella sometimes – her funny doodles, her impersonations of people. She was just annoyed at all the meanness that went along with the fun.

Evie poked around her salad with her fork. She wasn't sure how to ask to go to Maryam's house after this conversation, or whether she even wanted to. She barely knew Maryam, who seemed a little *too* keen to hang out. Plus, if Maryam suddenly started acting like they were best pals at school, things could get awkward. She let her mum ask Zac about his day. He described a game they played in PE in forensic detail, which gave Evie space to think.

Her mind went to her red folder. She couldn't just let a discovery like this go. She really did want to have a proper look at Maryam's folder, and it would be better to do it outside of school. Evie, having made her decision, jumped on a pause in conversation.

'Hey, Dad said I could hang out with a friend on Saturday. That's OK, right?' she asked.

'Remember, you've got piano in the morning,' Mum said. 'But then I guess that's OK. Which friend?'

'A new one,' Evie said. Her parents looked at each other, and she could tell they would need more information to be satisfied. 'Her name is . . .' Evie tried to think of a name that lots of people had. 'Sarah.'

'I don't remember anyone from your school called Sarah,' her mum said sceptically. 'Can she come here, as we've never met her before?'

'She didn't go to our primary school,' Evie said, thinking on her feet. Especially after this conversation, Maryam's house would be safer. 'And her mum is using the car on Saturday so she said it's easier if I go there. Besides, Dad *already said* it was fine.'

'Did I?' Dad asked, looking confused.

'Yup, just before you got on the phone,' Evie said.

'Well, OK,' Mum said reluctantly, shooting a look at Dad. 'I'll drop you off.'

Evie took a bite of lasagne. Now she just needed to get Maryam to be Sarah. She'd tell her in form time.

DELHI, INDIA

1929

9. Safia

Safia looked across the fabrics laid on a sheet on the floor of their flat, the big rolls lined up and stacked on top of one another in a system only Amma knew, ready for her brothers to carry them down to the shop. She didn't know why anyone would choose the simple white muslin Amma was now wrapping in paper instead of something more beautiful, like the turquoise-and-pink prints or glittering gold leaves that sat at the top of the stack, glinting in the dappled sun that shone through the shutters.

But Mrs Hollins had ordered what she had ordered, which was a simple white muslin dress. Amma had taken one of Mrs Hollins's old dresses to get the style and proportions right, as she wasn't accustomed to making western clothes. She'd worked on it every night for two weeks – Mrs Hollins had offered a price far beyond what Amma would have considered charging, and Amma wanted a satisfied customer.

'*Please* be careful, Safia,' Amma pleaded. 'Go straight there and give this to Anjali. And take the back alley.'

'Don't worry, I will,' Safia assured her, taking the parcel and heading downstairs. She pulled her *dupatta* over her head and turned onto the dim back alley so she wouldn't be seen out on her own. Once she was a few blocks away she crossed over to the dusty main road, navigating her way between the people carrying large woven baskets on their heads and the donkeys and camels dragging big, wooden carts. She was proud to be trusted with an important errand and knew she was foolish for disobeying instructions. Yet, she couldn't resist seeing the street alive with morning activity – even if it wasn't appropriate for a girl to be out, unaccompanied, amongst men.

It was only early in the day, but the street was busy and blazing hot. In the distance, she could see a wagon lumbering down the road, one man dumping water onto the street from a bucket and another mopping behind him. Knowing she'd never be able to keep the parcel dry, she crossed over to the other side, where a roof covered the path and created some shade.

She passed the wrought iron gates that surrounded St James' Church, its yellow and white dome poking from behind the trees like a giant *gulab jamun*. The thought of the sweet, syrupy dessert made her hungry, but she pressed on. Kathy often had some bit of candy in her pocket, which Safia pretended not to want but looked forward to.

She was so lost in thought about the caramel or peppermint that Kathy might share with her that it took her a moment to make out the figure leaning against a concrete wall, her yellow bicycle propped up next to her, waving. It was Kathy.

After the riot in front of the mosque last month, Kathy had stayed away for a week, but it wasn't long before she'd started sneaking back to Safia's neighbourhood whilst Anjali did her chores. Safia now expected her to come round most days, and felt disappointed when Kathy didn't show.

Allahu akbar!

The call to prayer rang out, and the crowd began

moving as one, towards the mosque. The remarkably clear and strong voice of the muezzin carried from the minaret right down the street.

Allahu akbar!

Kathy's ringlets had gone frizzy around her head, and her face was rosy and freckled. She looked hot despite wearing a light muslin dress, similar to the one her mother had ordered. Kathy stepped forward, grabbed Safia's sleeve and tugged her towards the bicycle. When she spoke, it was in a conspiratorial whisper, her blue eyes shining with excitement.

'Now's the time to do it, when all of the servants are at mosque.' She swung her leg over the seat of the bike and nodded at the back, but Safia wasn't sure what to do. 'Go on – just hop on the back!'

Allahhu akbar! Allahu Akbar!

Safia looked sceptically at the metal rack behind the seat. 'Kathy, wait,' she protested feebly. 'I must take this dress to your mother and I promise . . .' She halted, trying to get the English tense right. 'I promised that I would go directly there.' But her slow sentence got lost in the noise of a passing horse-drawn carriage laden with people and Kathy kicked the kickstand up. 'Don't worry. We're heading back to Civil Lines. It's on the way home.'

Safia wondered what was on the way home, but it was easier to follow than to argue, and she gingerly raised herself onto the back of the bike and hung onto Kathy's warm waist. Kathy began to pedal, and as she gathered speed Safia felt the wind lifting her *dupatta* behind her, creating a waving strip of green fabric.

Soon the streets became leafier and less busy as they crossed into the Civil Lines neighbourhood, where Kathy lived. They passed a big park, and the residential landscape around them was lined with large trees in front of walls and gates, and behind those, elegant bungalows where the British civil servants lived. Kathy abruptly pressed her brakes and put her foot down, sending Safia bumping into her back. They were in front of a brick wall, surrounding a large brick house. Safia suspected what it was Kathy wanted her to do, but hoped she was wrong.

'So,' Kathy said, 'you need to get as close as possible to the wall here so you can give me a lift over. I'll have a good look around, and take some mangoes for us.'

Safia groaned. 'I do not think this is a good idea.' If

they'd been speaking in Urdu, she would have unleashed a string of reasons: she was already late, if they got caught, *she* would get in much worse trouble than Kathy, and the mangoes at her uncle's stall were actually better. But in English, she just couldn't find the words fast enough.

Kathy pulled a small mirror from her satchel and held it at a tilt so she could see just over the other side of the wall. Safia saw a garden, and beyond that, a brick house in a style that mixed English and Indian, with its windows and doorways shaped into pointed arches, its walls covered in vegetation and its white balconies just visible.

By the wall was a wooden crate.

'Good, the crate is still there,' Kathy said. 'I'll toss the mangoes to you, so make sure you catch them!'

Safia shifted her weight from one foot to the other nervously. 'I'm not sure this is wise,' she said.

'Oh, don't be so lily-livered.'

'Lily . . . livered?' Safia frowned. It was a phrase that made no sense to her.

'It means chicken. Er . . . not being brave. I'll cover colloquialisms in our next English lesson,' Kathy said impatiently. 'For now, just give me a boost, please.' She walked over to the wall and Safia followed, putting her parcel down gently on the ground before holding out her hands for Kathy's foot in its brown leather Mary Jane. Safia heaved the girl up, and watched as she expertly swung her legs over the wall and came down with a thump. 'I'm over!' she said.

Safia heard rustling and could just see the top of Kathy's head as she wandered around the garden. She didn't seem to be in a hurry, and paused at the pink hibiscus flowers, breaking one off and putting it behind her ear. Safia looked around nervously, but the street was empty. Kathy eventually made her way to the mango tree and called, 'There is a nice one on the ground. I'm going to toss it over.'

'I am ready,' Safia said in her halting English. A fat mango then came sailing over the wall in a beautiful arc, and Safia quickly thought to spread out the long shirt of her *kurta* to catch it. It landed squarely in the middle with a satisfying bounce. 'I have it!' she called back with joy. It was purplish-green and felt perfectly ripe.

'Good! That one can be yours,' Kathy said. Safia could hear her beginning to climb the tree, grunting as she grabbed for a branch and pulled herself up. Safia could see her clearly now, reaching for a mango with one freckled hand. She picked it, and swung down with the other hand.

'Here comes another!' Kathy shouted. Safia shielded her eyes from the sun as she looked for the mango in the air. But it came too low, and shallowly made it over the wall. Safia had to scurry forward for it, but she was too far away. She leaped forward and hit the brick wall with her palms just as it plopped on the pavement with a squelch. She closed her eyes for a moment before she dared look down. The mango had landed right next to the parcel, splattering orange pulp all over the thin paper. Safia softly banged her forehead on the wall, cursing under her breath.

'Oops!' Kathy said, hearing the splat. 'Poor throw, sorry!'

Safia squatted down, a knot of fear growing in her belly, and frantically tried to wipe the pulp off the brown paper with her shirt. But it was no good – the neatly wrapped package was covered. Carefully, she unwrapped the paper to check the damage. Perhaps it was just the outside, she told herself. Perhaps the dress was fine. But her eyes began to burn with tears when she saw two bright orange splotches on the gauzy, white fabric of the dress. They were each only the size of a grape, but as bright as goldfish.

Selfish Kathy, never thinking of anyone else, she thought savagely.

There was the sound of a heavy door swinging open. Safia heard Kathy scuttle towards the wall, turn the crate on its side and climb onto it. Her hands appeared over the top of the wall just as the crate cracked with a loud crunch under her feet.

'Miss Kathy, are you in the garden again?' a heavily accented woman's voice called. Safia could just see the woman, wearing a sari, poke her head around the carved wooden door. 'The councillor has said that you are not to go in his garden!'

Safia's anger at Kathy evaporated with the threat of being caught. Safia wanted to run, knowing the councillor's maid would make sure she was punished if she was seen. But she didn't want to leave Kathy, now gracelessly shimmying one leg over the wall, on her own.

Kathy managed to shift her belly onto the wall and then swing the other leg over. She dropped heavily down, landing on her feet. The woman in the sari was still shouting, 'Miss Kathy, I will need to tell the councillor if this happens again!'

Kathy giggled, oblivious to the tears running down Safia's cheeks, and got back on her bike. Safia once again hopped on the back, clutching the ruined parcel with one hand and Kathy's waist with the other. She held in her sobs, but felt like she couldn't get enough air into her lungs, and rested her forehead on Kathy's back, gasping.

Kathy skidded her foot across the ground, finally noticing Safia was upset and stopping the bike. She turned to Safia with concern. 'What is it, Safia? Whatever is the matter?'

Safia held out the stained dress in her hands, choking out the words, 'My mother . . . worked so hard . . . I promised.'

Kathy looked down at the stain and then back up at Safia, understanding. 'Don't worry,' she said calmly. 'It was my fault entirely. I shall make it right.'

'How?' Safia asked. She hoped there was an obvious solution.

'I said don't worry,' Kathy said. 'Just trust me.' Despite Kathy's confidence, Safia could see her eyes darting around, trying to think of what to do, and Safia grew anxious again when she realised that Kathy did not, in fact, have a plan.

But then something seemed to click for Kathy and she began pedalling again with purpose, back towards the busy streets of Old Delhi. Safia sniffed and wiped her eyes on her sleeves, keeping her head down so no one would see her red nose. Kathy finally stopped just inside the old city gate, at the stand of Farooq, the *lassi* man and Naeem's father. Naeem prepared to ladle them a little sip for free – a benefit of friendship that Kathy cashed in daily – while Farooq turned his back to avoid both this free sip and seeing Safia out on her own. But when Kathy took off her shoe, pulled out a coin, and handed it over, he couldn't help but turn around. Farooq raised his eyebrows and said, 'Big spender today, eh?' and scooped Kathy a tall brass cup of cool mango *lassi*. She took a long sip as Safia looked on in confusion. Then, she dumped the rest of the cup down the front of her dress.

Naeem looked at Safia, mouth agape, who threw her hands up in bewilderment. Watching Kathy waste a whole cup of *lassi* on a hot day was almost physically painful.

'What's wrong with you?' she whispered to Kathy.

'Just trust me, OK?' Kathy said. '*Shukria!*' she said to Farooq and Naeem, using one of the three Urdu words she knew, and turned her bike around again. Safia looked back at Naeem and shrugged, having little other choice than to go along, back towards Civil Lines. They went up a different road this time, past the Christian cemetery with its ominous white cross, and Safia began to feel nauseous. She thought about her mother, who had so wanted to prove herself as a good seamstress to Mrs Hollins, measuring everything out perfectly, unpicking stitches and re-doing them when they weren't perfect. She wasn't sure if she was angrier at Kathy or herself.

The bike rolled to a stop in front of the white stucco wall that Safia knew to belong to Kathy's family. Kevan, the guard, stood in front of the metal gate, which he unlatched and opened for Kathy, raising an eyebrow as he glanced at Safia.

'Hello, Kay-von!'

Safia winced at Kathy's pronunciation and looked at the ground as she followed Kathy through the gate.

Entering the gate was like entering an oasis. A broad, green lawn stretched out in front of her, with manicured plants around the edge of the cream-coloured concrete house. The house was surrounded by a covered patio held up by columns, and had windows framed by arches. Safia thought it looked like something from Ancient Greece.

They went around the side of the house where a small table and two chairs sat on the lawn. Anjali poured tea from a porcelain pot with pink roses on it into a matching cup. The woman holding the cup, who was sitting at a small table laid with a white tablecloth, was Mrs Hollins – Kathy's mother. She wore her blonde hair pinned up under a wide-brimmed straw hat. Her dress was of the same white, lightweight material as Kathy's, but hers had long sleeves and a more fitted waist, and went down nearly to her ankles. When she looked up, her gaze went immediately to the bright orange stain that covered the entire front of Kathy's dress and her brow furrowed deeply. She glanced briefly at Safia by her side and the furrow seemed to deepen further.

She placed the scone with jam she had been nibbling at back on its dainty plate, as if readying herself to get angry. Safia cast her eyes down at the grass beneath her sandals, feeling herself shrink in the face of Mrs Hollins's glare.

'Katherine, I've no idea how you manage to make such a thorough mess of yourself every single time you are out of my sight,' she said in a low voice. To Safia, it sounded worse than anger – it sounded like complete disdain.

'I'm sorry, Mother,' Kathy said, her eyes lowered in false repentance. 'I met Safia in the street, and she was coming to deliver this dress to you, when a bicycle driver crashed into the stand next to us and spilled mango *lassi* everywhere.' Kathy took the parcel from Safia's hands. 'It's gotten on your new dress as well,' she said, bringing the parcel to her mother.

Safia saw what Kathy was doing and held her breath while she waited to see if it would work.

'Oh, well that's just fine!' Kathy's mother said sarcastically, pulling at the fabric of the new dress with two fingers, as if it was an old dishrag. 'Anjali, will you be able to do anything with this?'

Anjali held the dress in front of her and let it fall to its full length to inspect it. She looked at Safia out of the corner of her eye with disapproval. Safia met her gaze with a pleading expression, hoping Anjali was on her side. 'Yes, ma'am, I think so. I will try with Miss Katherine's as well.'

'Thank you,' Mrs Hollins said in a lazy drawl. Turning back to Kathy she said, 'Go take that fouled thing off and get changed. You have your art lesson soon.' Then, glancing at Safia, she said in a clipped voice, 'The girl must go now.'

In all the times Safia had met Mrs Hollins, she'd never been asked her name. But she was more than happy to be dismissed from the tense scene.

'Yes, Mother,' Kathy replied. Then, looking meek once again, she said, 'Safia's mother will just need payment for the dress.'

Safia let her held breath out, too nervous to keep it in any longer. Anjali's eyes went sharply to her, as if urging her not to draw attention to herself.

Mrs Hollins took another sip of tea and looked down her nose at Safia. 'I'm not sure it's entirely fair that I pay the full price for a dress that may very well be ruined.'

Safia's heart sped, and she wiped her palms anxiously on the front of her shirt. She knew how unhappy Amma would be if she didn't get paid the full amount. She'd worked hard, and the whole family was relying on that payment.

'Mother, please,' Kathy cut in. 'She wasn't to blame. If anything, it was my fault for stopping her to chat to me.'

Safia could have hugged her. It was the best she could do, beyond not stealing those silly mangoes in the first place. She just hoped it would be enough.

Kathy's mother looked somewhat sceptical, but said, 'Very well then. Anjali, please fetch the money to give the girl. Kathy, I'll deduct half of that from your pocket money.'

Safia turned her eyes towards Kathy without looking up and saw her wince. But all she said was, 'Thank you, Mother.'

Safia didn't dare look at Kathy, lest her mother see and think it was a plan between them. She just looked back down at her feet, her heart still thumping but her limbs light with relief.

Anjali walked briskly across the lawn, her blue sari flowing behind her, and came back with the rupees, which she pressed into Safia's hand. 'Be careful,' she said, and her eyes were full of warning. Safia nodded and walked fast, nearly jogging, back towards the gate and past Kevan, her sandals clapping against the soles of her feet and her heart full of affection for her friend.

10. *Kathy*

Once she was out of her mother's sight, Kathy allowed her steps to stamp – down the portico, through the side door, and across the cool corridor to her bedroom. Her face burned with annoyance, half at her mother and half at herself. Safia had been right, of course – she never should have stolen those mangoes. In her room, she pulled open the shutters to let the light in. She knew it would irritate her mother, who insisted on keeping them closed to keep the rooms cool.

Anjali appeared in the doorway, wearing her usual anxious expression, her eyes moving to the shutters and then back to Kathy.

'How much do I owe?' Kathy asked despondently.

'Five rupees,' Anjali said. Kathy went to the vanity and

took a velvet drawstring bag from the drawer, her heart lightening that her savings wouldn't be so depleted after all. But was Safia's mother really only charging ten rupees for a dress she'd worked on for a fortnight? She counted out the coins and handed them to Anjali. But rather than go, Anjali lingered in the doorway.

'Miss Kathy, I am not sure,' she started, 'but I think you just did a kind thing for Safia.' Kathy opened her mouth to speak, but Anjali held up her hand. 'You are a good person, Kathy, but you must remember that things are different for Safia than for you.'

Kathy waited for her to explain, but she picked up her hamper of laundry and walked back down the corridor. She knew Anjali was right – she was always getting herself into trouble, and it wasn't fair to drag Safia along. But she'd made it right this time. Bandar sat at the window and she undid the latch and let him in. The monkey leaped from her bed to her desk, then settled on her shoulder, picking through her hair with his little hands.

She promised herself to be better in the future, but wondered if she could keep that promise when there was so much fun to be had.

*

Kathy changed into a clean dress, gathered her art supplies and headed to the back garden. Miss Kerridge was setting up her easel. Ruth sat on a wicker chair, her ankles crossed and her hands folded in her lap. Her chocolate brown hair was pulled into a flawless plait. Kathy instinctively smoothed her own hair down, but could feel it frizz back up immediately.

She sat on the other chair, leaving a good gap between herself and Ruth. Miss Kerridge positioned a bowl of fruit on the table in front of them, shifting it slightly to catch the light differently, then giving a little nod of satisfaction. *More fruit*, Kathy lamented to herself, and sighed involuntarily. Miss Kerridge looked up sharply.

Kathy knew she was lucky that her parents paid for art classes with Miss Kerridge, but she thought she might go completely barmy if she had to draw another banana.

As if reading her mind, Miss Kerridge said, 'I shall be happy to move on to a different subject once you have mastered this one, Miss Hollins.' Kathy noticed a small patch of sweat on the back of her teacher's shirt and felt a twinge of pity for her.

'Oh, I've forgotten my charcoal,' Miss Kerridge said with a frown. 'Do pardon me, girls. Please have a go at sketching the fruit until I return.' Her skirts rustled as she hurried back into the house.

Once she'd left, Ruth asked in a coy voice, 'So will you miss me when I'm back in England?' She directed the comment at her sketchbook, where she started to sketch the outline of a mango.

Kathy put her pencil down and looked at Ruth, trying to determine if she was joking. 'Sorry?'

'Did your mother not tell you?'

Kathy shook her head. *Obviously* her mother hadn't told her. She wished Ruth would just come out with it. She pulled a pistachio from her pocket and lobbed it towards Ruth's ankles. Bandar jumped down from the porch railing and snatched it greedily, making Ruth jump back in disgust. 'You're moving to England?'

'Yes,' Ruth said, composing herself and returning to her mango. 'Next month.'

'Why?' Kathy had a vague sense that they would all go back to England eventually, but the idea had seemed far away.

'Mother says that the time has come for me to be educated properly.'

Why was the time suddenly coming for things to change? She still felt like the same person she'd been last year, and Ruth was certainly just as obnoxious as she'd always been. Yet, something seemed to be shifting in how the adults saw them. Kathy wondered with panic if she'd be shipped to England next. The thought of it made Kathy feel frightened. She imagined it was all the things in life she hated – art lessons, starched dresses, cutlery.

'When do you leave?' Kathy asked.

'In a fortnight,' Ruth replied. Kathy could hear the slightest wobble in her otherwise confident voice. But she soon steadied it again. 'No time to dwell, though. There's so much to do.'

Kathy clung to the wobble. She wanted Ruth to admit the truth: she was scared. 'Are you frightened?' Kathy asked. 'I mean, to move somewhere new on your own?'

Ruth smoothed her skirt down with her palms. 'Oh no. Not really,' she said. Ruth spoke more quickly now, and sounded less confident, as if she was reassuring herself. 'Mother says I'll make lots of dear friends in no time. She says I'll fit right in, and no one will ever guess I came from India.'

Kathy could hear that Ruth was reciting a script, and trying to convince herself of it. She felt bad for her. This was something they'd all been raised to feel anxious about – whether they were English enough. Whether they seemed Indian. And yet, this was their home. In a way, they *were* Indian.

Miss Kerridge came back, even dewier than before.

'My apologies, girls,' she said, dabbing her brow and coming round to inspect their sketches. Kathy hadn't even picked up her pencil, and hastily opened her sketchbook to a random page to at least look like she'd tried.

Miss Kerridge took the book off her. 'Fantastic, Kathy,' she beamed. 'The shading is just magnificent.' Puzzled, Kathy accepted the book back. 'Ruth,' their teacher continued, 'I think you could have made more of an effort.'

Kathy looked down in confusion to see an expertly sketched banana on the page. Its skin was realistically mottled, and it cast a perfectly sized shadow beneath it. It was, unmistakably, Safia's.

LONDON, UK

PRESENT DAY

11. A Playdate

Maryam doodled an eye, giving special attention to the thin lines of the iris, to give herself something to do at the start of form time. She was relieved and apprehensive that Evie was perching on Arabella's desk – relieved because she wasn't quite sure how to interact with Evie in public, and apprehensive because anyone close to Arabella was somewhat suspicious. Mr Whipple started to get up from his desk, and Evie returned to her seat, nonchalantly dropping a scrap of paper at Maryam's desk on the way.

I can come to yours on Saturday.

Maryam's stomach turned over. She'd never had a friend over from school before. Her flat didn't seem to have enough space to have any additional people in it, and anyway her parents had never seemed too keen on organising anything with her primary school friends.

For the first time, Maryam wondered if this was because they were embarrassed about where they lived. She imagined that Evie lived in one of the big houses on the hill, with a front garden and a back garden, and a door with stained glass panels. She imagined her telling her friends that she'd gone on a field trip to the wild world of Grimsby.

She wrote a response on the note: *OK. Can we go to yours instead?*

She wasn't quite sure how to pass the note back discreetly, but also didn't want Evie to realise that she'd never passed a note before. She waited for Mr Whipple to turn his back and hurriedly threw it across. The note glided off the table and Evie reached down to get it, rolling her eyes. She wrote a response and passed it back.

All it said, without explanation, was: *No, sorry.*

Mr Whipple had written a discussion question on the board, and the sounds of chairs scraping and people chattering started to rise in the classroom. Evie pulled her chair around to Maryam and carried on their exchange from the note.

'There's just one thing,' she said, pausing and running her tongue across the front of her mouth, making her top lip bulge out. 'You . . . have to pretend you're called Sarah.'

Maryam furrowed her brow in confusion. 'Why?'

'Um.' Evie hesitated, looking increasingly uncomfortable and rubbing the palms of her hands against her skirt. 'My mum sort of heard about the thing with Bella.'

Maryam's heart raced in panic. How had Evie's mum heard? Did everyone else's parents know each other? She suddenly felt she couldn't look Evie in the face. Now all the posh parents would think she was a bad kid, and probably half the teachers too. She closed her eyes tight, so frustrated with how unfair it was, and how quickly that one little hiss had spread.

Evie pulled in closer and said, 'I told my mum it wasn't your fault. Seriously, I did.' She spoke in a low voice. 'But I just wasn't sure she'd let me go if I told her you were *that* Maryam.'

What had felt like the start of a friendship now felt like a business transaction. You can't be friends with someone if they don't even use your real name, can you? But it wasn't Evie's fault, really.

'I get it,' Maryam said, composing herself. 'So, what time do you want to come over?'

Evie's face relaxed. 'How about two? You can text me your address.'

'I'd better just write it down,' Maryam said, scribbling on a sheet from her notebook. It was breaktime, and as Evie streamed out with the others, Maryam dawdled in the classroom until she had no choice but to leave.

That Saturday was bright and chilly. Maryam stood at the window, looking out below for Evie and her mum, who would be arriving any moment. She could see Hassan and Lennox sitting on a bench in the courtyard, both wearing puffy black jackets with the hoods of their sweatshirts pulled up, sharing a bag of hot chips from the chicken shop. Hassan was imitating someone from their class and Lennox cracked up, chips spilling out of his mouth.

Maryam busied herself tidying as she waited. She went into the corridor, straightened the shoes scattered across the entryway, and took away a cold mug of tea from the sideboard. But by the time she'd brought one mug to the sink, Nani had left another on the dining table.

Suddenly remembering something, she raced out the door, down the stairs, and to the bench.

'Guys,' she said, out of breath, 'when Evie comes, you have to pretend my name is Sarah.'

'What? Why?' Hassan asked.

'I'll explain later, but please just do it!' Maryam pleaded. Lennox chuckled to himself.

'You got yourself in deep, man,' he said.

'Stop calling me man,' Maryam said. 'It's Sarah, OK?'

'OK, boss,' Lennox said.

Just then, an arm in a wool coat wiggled through the gate and waved.

'Hey, Sarah,' Evie called, making eye contact to make sure Maryam remembered who she was meant to be.

'Hi!' Maryam said, jogging over. 'Hang on, I'll let you in.'

Evie and her mum stood on the other side of the gate in the fence that surrounded the block of flats and court-yard. Maryam felt her stomach knot up. Evie's mum held her car keys in her hand and darted her eyes around, taking in the surroundings. Her gaze stopped on Hassan and Lennox. She looked anxious.

Trying to show some manners, Maryam welcomed them in through the courtyard. Seeing it through Evie's mum's eyes, she now noticed the patchy, brown grass, the bottlecaps, the bits of plastic wrapper being blown around.

'This is my brother, Hassan, and his friend, Lennox,' Maryam said, gesturing towards the boys and then leading Evie and her mum upstairs.

'Is there . . . an adult at home?' Evie's mum asked with suspicion, still looking all around. Maryam could tell she didn't like the idea of leaving Evie here.

'Yes, my grandmother is inside.' But, turning the handle, Maryam realised with dread that she had let the door close behind her and was now locked out. She thought she saw Evie's mum flash her a look. 'Nani!' she shouted, banging. 'Can you let me in?'

When there was no response, she banged again, and turned to Evie's mum, embarrassed, explaining, 'She's a bit hard of hearing and sometimes she puts the TV on too loud.'

Finally, they heard shuffling coming towards the door, and Nani appeared. Maryam could see Evie's mum looking at this old woman wearing a *salwar kameez* with a dressing gown over the top, and imagined she was wondering whether she was really going to entrust her daughter to her care.

'Hello!' Nani said brightly. 'Come in, come in.' She turned and walked back into the living room, expecting everyone to follow. 'And which friend is this?' she asked, looking at Evie. Maryam was very grateful that Nani was making it sound like she had friends round often.

'Hello, I'm Evie. Pleased to meet you,' she said politely. 'Thank you for having me over.'

Maryam realised that she hadn't told Nani that her name was meant to be Sarah, and felt annoyed at herself for making this basic mistake. She just knew that Nani would mention her name if she didn't quickly wrap up the conversation.

'OK, well we'd better get to work on that project,' Maryam said.

'Ah, Mari is always working so hard,' Nani said. Evie's mum furrowed her brow and looked at Maryam.

'You're Sarah, aren't you?' she asked.

Maryam's heart sped up. 'Yes. My family has lots of

nicknames though.' She put her arm around Nani and guided her over to the sofa. 'OK, Nani, I think your programme is on now!'

'Which one?' Nani looked confused.

'I'll find it for you in just a second,' Maryam said, turning back to Evie and her mum.

Evie's mum seemed to have made the decision to let Evie stay, and now she appeared eager to extract herself.

'OK, Evie, so I'll be back in an hour,' her mum said.

'An hour? Can't I stay a bit longer?'

'No, I'm sorry. We have lots to do later today.' Her mum shot her a stern look that said that it wasn't open for argument. 'Be ready to go in an hour, OK?'

'OK,' Evie said, defeated.

Once her mum left, Evie and Maryam went into the bedroom and took out their folders. They realised at that moment that they didn't have a plan, and they only had an hour together. Maryam stepped out to the railing and called down to Hassan.

'Please come up! We need help!' Maryam begged.

Hassan flung his head back on the bench as if this was asking a great sacrifice.

'Better go make sure your sister's not getting played,' Lennox said loudly, as he strolled away across the courtyard. Maryam's face grew hot. She hoped Evie hadn't heard.

Hassan pulled himself upright and dragged himself towards the stairs. 'We need your phone,' he said to Evie when he got to the landing. 'Let's go inside. It's freezing out here.'

Back inside, they spread out all the pages on the carpet and Maryam wiped the fog off her glasses. They counted five letters in each of the folders. The first letter in Evie's was addressed to 'Brkyp' and signed 'Jrwzr'. In Maryam's it was the opposite, to 'Jrwzr', from 'Brkyp'. But after the first ones, there were no greetings and no names signed.

'So it looks like … burk-yip and … jur-wuz-ur are people?' Hassan asked, struggling to say the names. 'But who are they?'

'We don't know. My friend Zoe thinks it looks like Finnish.'

'I thought you didn't tell anyone,' Maryam retorted. Evie had seemed so annoyed that she'd told Hassan, but now that Zoe knew, this would get around to half the kids

in the school. Maryam didn't mind too much though –
maybe someone could help them solve it.

'Oh, I . . . just told her yesterday.'

Maryam was already forming the distinct impression
that Evie wasn't the best liar.

'Finnish . . .' Hassan said with puzzlement, looking at
one of the pages. 'Can I use your phone?' Hassan asked
Evie.

'Um, OK,' she said, sounding a little reluctant. 'Do you
not have a computer?'

'No,' Maryam said. She hoped Hassan would come up
with a good idea, because at the moment she didn't feel
like she had much to add to this partnership.

'How do you even do your homework?' Evie asked.

'We use the library when we need one,' Maryam
explained, growing impatient. 'You can watch everything
we do on it. You'll be right here. OK?'

Evie, convinced, put in her passcode while shielding
the phone from view and handed it over. Hassan first
went to a search engine and put in *Uvri translation*.

'These two start with "Uvri",' he explained. 'So it
seems like that must mean "dear" in whatever language it

140

is.' Maryam swelled with pride. She knew Hassan would know what to do.

He frowned. 'All that comes back is the . . . Uganda Virus Research Institute.'

'What's that?' Maryam asked.

'It looks like they research viruses,' Hassan said, then added needlessly, 'in Uganda.' Maryam's eyebrows raised at this. Could they have been part of a secret research project? But Hassan shut down the thought. 'Anyhow, it wasn't founded until 2001.'

'But what about "Family Recipes"? That has to mean something, right?' Evie asked. Maryam and Hassan agreed that it seemed cryptic, but a search for the phrase just gave them recipes.

Hassan took his chemistry textbook down from the shelf and flipped to the periodic table. 'Maybe they're elements,' he muttered to himself. 'U is uranium, V is vanadium , I is iodine. . . but there's no R . . .'

'Oh, hey,' Maryam cut in, 'there's something I forgot to tell you. Nani's mum and Evie's great-grandmother were both born in Delhi!'

'What?'

Evie took out her family tree homework, which she'd tucked into her red folder. Maryam unfolded it on the carpet.

Hassan scanned the big, colourful tree. 'You going for extra credit or something, Evie?' His finger stopped on the box that said *Katherine Hollins: B. 1918, Delhi*. He then started typing furiously into Evie's phone.

Evie ignored his comment. 'What are you searching for?'

'Just looking for what this lady Katherine got up to,' he said, scrolling with a frown. 'But there are a *lot* of people named Katherine Hollins.'

'Well, I know her father was in the army. And she . . . lived in Cambridge? She was a teacher?'

He typed quickly with his thumbs, scrolled, and then stopped. He turned the phone around to display an announcement of the wedding of Katherine Hollins and Gordon Armitage from an old newspaper that someone had put on a site about Cambridge local history. The image was grainy, but Maryam looked at Katherine's pin-curled hair and lace dress, the jewelled pendant hanging round her neck, and thought she and the lanky, moustachioed man in the photo looked like the epitome of rich people from the 1930s.

'She really doesn't look like she was born in India,' Maryam said. It was such an obvious statement that she felt silly for saying it.

'There were loads of white British people in India back then. Colonialism and all that,' Hassan said dismissively, and before Maryam could think through what he meant, he continued, 'And what was she doing during the Second World War?'

'Why? What does that have to do with our folders?' Maryam cut in.

'Look at the dates on the pages,' he said. Maryam looked across the sheets and couldn't believe she hadn't noticed that the letters were dated. The earliest was from 1942 and the latest from 1947. Of course – that was mostly during the Second World War, which supported the idea that this was some kind of code. But what could that have to do with her great-grandmother Safia?

'Um,' Evie looked up at the ceiling, thinking. 'I dunno. I think her husband was in the army and fought in France?' She mouthed silently as she counted backwards. 'It would have been just before my gran was born.'

They each sat in silence, leafing through the letters to

busy their hands, as if a clue might somehow pop off the page. Was Nani's mum a spy? Or a scientist? It was hard to believe that there might be anyone in her family with such an exciting job that they'd need to communicate in code. What was she trying to hide?

'We should go to Cambridge and talk to my gran,' Evie said. 'She might know something.'

Maryam noticed the 'we' in this sentence, first with excitement, and then with fear. She hadn't ever left London, let alone with someone else's family under a false identity. She wondered how they'd even get there, but didn't want to sound too ignorant by asking.

Just then, there was a knock at the door.

'Ugghh!' Evie groaned. 'It hasn't even been an hour!' she said, angry. She stamped to the front door, and waited while Maryam undid the lock for her. Evie's mum stood on the balcony, not making any motions to linger or come inside.

'Mum, you're early,' Evie said.

'Just a little,' her mum said gently, then turned to Maryam. 'Thanks for having Evie. We must have you over soon.'

'How about next weekend?' Evie piped in.

Her mum looked uncomfortable and fumbled with her keys. 'Um, we need to check our diary. Next weekend is busy.' She began to turn to go.

Hassan came out of the bedroom, handing Evie's phone over. Evie's mum frowned and looked at Evie, who took the phone and jammed it into the pocket of her bag. Maryam knew it would ring some kind of alarm bell that Hassan had been using Evie's phone.

'Bye, Sarah,' Evie said. 'I'll see you at school.'

'See you Monday,' Maryam said, shutting the door. Out the window, she saw Evie and her mum walk down the stairs to the courtyard, her mum still looking all around her.

12. A Close Call

Evie sat in the backseat, silently watching the housing estate and the blocks of flats around it float away.

'So, was it OK?' Mum asked, looking at her through the rearview mirror.

'Yeah, I had fun,' Evie said, slightly surprised that this was the truth – she hadn't been ready to go home.

They sat in silence for the rest of the very short drive home. As they pulled into a space on their road, Evie undid her seatbelt and hopped out. She waited on the doorstep. She could tell from the way her mum kept looking at her hesitantly that she wanted to talk, probably about Maryam and her brother.

Holding the keys to the house in her hand, Mum asked, 'Why did that boy have your phone?'

'Hassan? He was helping us do research,' Evie said, ready for the question. 'And he was interested in Gran's mum, who was born in India.'

Mum looked uncertain, but finally put the key in the door. Before she opened it, she looked Evie in the eye.

'I'm not going to take your phone to look at it. I'm going to trust you. But I want you to know that you can tell me anything, and I only want to keep you safe.'

'OK,' Evie said, looking at her feet. If Mum checked her phone, she might see some of the photos of Maryam that people had posted in the group chat with cat ears drawn on and realise who Sarah really was.

'I don't know this girl Sarah, and I don't know her family. All I know is that there didn't seem to be a lot of adult supervision, outside of this teenage boy who wants to hang out with his little sister's friends, which I find quite strange.'

'Her grandmother was there,' Evie came back defensively, 'and anyways, Hassan is nice.' The second the door opened, she went in and straight up the stairs to her room. Her face grew hot – at her mother's reaction, and at her inability to correct it.

Evie got out her phone, typed *Katherine Hollins Armitage* into the search bar, and studied the same grainy wedding announcement Hassan had found. The man was wearing a morning coat, holding a top hat, and had a skinny moustache like men in old fashioned movies. Katherine was wearing a white dress. Not a big fluffy ball gown, but a pretty and plain white dress, with a high neckline and a simple veil. A single jewel hung on a pendant. The date said 1938. The woman looked remarkably like her own mum, with her sharp nose and strong chin, but with her wavy hair cut short. Looking at the photo, it did indeed seem hard to believe that this woman could have been born in India, and even harder to imagine that she might have been friends with Maryam's great-grandmother.

Just then, Dad called up asking for help with dinner. Zoe and Bella were coming over with their parents, and she heard her own parents fussing about in the kitchen, getting out the nice plates and glasses. She put the folder away and started walking downstairs, but something in the hushed way her parents were speaking made her stop halfway down the stairs and listen in.

'Well, she's getting older. Maybe this is her way of rebelling,' Dad said.

'But I don't understand,' Mum replied, 'she has a great group of friends she's known most of her life. Why go looking for new ones in dodgy housing estates?'

Mum's whispers were much harder to catch than Dad's. He kept replying at a regular volume and Mum would shush him urgently.

'Maybe she wants friends whose parents aren't friends with us.'

'Well, that's just it. I don't know this girl, and there were no parents around. Just a grandmother who seemed not all there and a teenage brother who was hanging around the courtyard with his sketchy looking friend.'

Zac came up behind Evie, nudging her calf with his foot.

'What are you doing on the stairs?' he asked loudly.

Both her parents stopped speaking abruptly and looked up at the staircase, wondering if they had been heard. Evie went down, not answering Zac. Her parents scurried around the kitchen, pretending to stir the pans.

When Evie came into the kitchen, Mum and Dad looked at her, but she just filled up her water glass. She didn't think Maryam and Hassan were 'sketchy', but she knew she wouldn't be able to explain why. She changed the subject.

'Zac, have you finished your birthday list?' It was Zac's seventh birthday in two weeks, and perfecting his birthday list had been his obsession for the past month. Asking him about it would set off a twenty-minute conversation and buy her some headspace while she laid the table. Zac bounced in his seat.

'Almost! I want a superhero duvet, and a matching pillowcase, and a clicky pen with five colours like yours, and an ant farm, and a trampoline, and a chameleon.' Zac followed her around the table, as she tried to think of the right time to propose a trip to Cambridge, and the odds that they'd say yes to bringing her new friend.

Mum handed her a packet of the nice crisps and an open jar of olives and reached up into the cupboard to get out the fancy bowls – the ones from Amsterdam that looked like bird nests. Evie poured the snacks in.

'I'm sorry I was hard on your friend,' Mum said as she put the little bowls around the kitchen island. 'It sounds like you had a nice time today.'

Evie softened when she realised Mum was trying to apologise.

'That's OK,' Evie said. 'Her family isn't dodgy, you know.'

'OK,' Mum said. 'It's just that I don't know her. And I wonder if anything has happened with your old friends. You know, the Three Amigos.'

Evie thought about this, not sure of the answer herself.

'No, nothing *happened*,' Evie said. 'It's just that they're not always that nice.'

'You mean to you?' She saw Mum raise her eyebrows and prepare to protect her.

'No, they're fine to me. Just not to some of the other kids at school,' Evie said. Mum put her arm around Evie.

'It's normal to have ups and downs in friendship,' Mum said. 'But you've known these girls since you were toddlers. They're going to be your friends for life.'

Evie wondered if this was true. She leaned her head on Mum's arm, feeling the soft wool of her jumper against her cheek. She imagined herself living in this same part of North London, taking her children round for dinner with Auntie Bella and Auntie Zoe. There was something comforting about the thought, and about the idea of having friends for life. But the idea felt nicer than the reality of being friends with only them. She wondered if their children would also be competing over who was better at piano.

Mum gave her a squeeze. Evie wasn't sure whether her mum understood what she was thinking, but it was nice to be close to her and smell her perfume. Evie was brave enough to ask.

'So,' she started, 'are we going to visit Gran before Christmas?'

'Maybe we'll go up for Boxing Day,' Mum said.

'Could we go next weekend?' Evie came back quickly. Mum pulled back a bit, looking surprised.

'Oh, I don't know.' Mum hesitated. 'Things are really busy at the moment.'

'But I want to interview Gran for my family tree project, and it's due at the end of term,' Evie protested. Her mum considered it. It was hard for her to say no to a school project.

'I suppose we could.'

Evie knew that the hardest part was yet to come.

'And, another thing. We're supposed to learn about our partner's family. So can I bring my partner?'

Evie waited tensely as her mum considered this.

'That seems a bit extreme for a school project. Is everyone travelling to each other's families?'

'No,' Evie thought fast, 'but we thought it would be more interesting to meet the actual people. Like, investigative journalism.' Evie thought her mum, who was always encouraging her to think about different careers, would like that last bit. She saw that she was right.

'And who's your partner?' Mum asked.

'Sarah,' Evie said. She saw Mum shoot a look of concern at Dad and then go back to stirring the gravy.

'I think I'm going to need to talk to Sarah's parents about this.'

'OK,' Evie replied with pretend nonchalance, wondering with panic how she'd navigate their parents meeting each other.

The doorbell went and it was Zoe and her family, and then, five minutes later, Bella and her parents. Everyone shuffled into the open-plan kitchen and Evie's dad passed around glasses of wine for the parents and lemonades for the children.

'You girls can go and play in the garden until it's dinnertime,' Dad said. 'Avoid the boring adult chat, eh?' he said, smiling at the three of them.

Evie led Zoe and Bella out of the back door, and they gravitated towards the playhouse. They were too old for it now, but they climbed up onto the roof.

'What's new?' Evie asked.

'I finally got my cat yesterday,' Bella said, beaming. She had been promised a kitten at the start of the year but it had taken a while to adopt one. 'Her name is Cookie.' She pulled out her phone to look for a photo while she chattered away. 'She's a Balinese, so she's really fluffy.'

'She's *very* cute,' Zoe confirmed, and for a moment Evie felt a little left out that Zoe had already met her.

'Mogyam's not the only cat in town any more!' Bella said with a mean smile.

Evie accepted the phone and scrolled through photos of the round little ball of fluff with two shiny eyes. It was indeed exceptionally cute.

The back door to the kitchen was open and Evie could hear snippets of conversation, music, and occasional laughter. She leaned back on the roof of the playhouse, looking across the rows of back fences stretching to the end of their block. It was only late afternoon, but the sun was setting, casting a bright, peachy light across the sky. Bella was talking about how Cookie lost her mind when you shone a light on the floor. Then, she heard something from inside that made her ears prick up.

'This girl, Maryam, it sounds like she's been exhibiting classic bullying behaviour,' Mum said.

'I know, but I can't be seen to be disciplining her too harshly,' Ms Underhill said, 'considering my position.'

The conversation then moved on to some television programme.

Evie fumed, wondering what version of the story Bella had told her parents.

'Evie, what do you think?' Bella asked.

'Huh?'

'We just asked if you want to do a group act for St Mary's Got Talent next term?' Bella waved a hand across her face. 'Earth to Evie!' she laughed.

'Your face has gone crimson all of a sudden,' Zoe added. 'Are you OK?'

'Yeah, I'm fine. Sure. Group act for the talent show sounds good.' She forced a small smile.

Dad called them inside for dinner and they took their places around a folding table next to the dining room table, where the adults sat. Evie thought they were getting a little old to sit at the kids table, but there wasn't anywhere else for them to go. Zac and Hector, Zoe's little brother, had a sword fight with their knives. Evie's dad passed around plates of roast chicken with potatoes and vegetables. He left a small pitcher of gravy on the table, and Zac poured it all over his plate until the food was swimming in it.

'Zac, that's gross,' Evie said.

'That's how I like it!' he said, scooping it up with his spoon and slurping it down hungrily. The others wrinkled their noses in disgust.

'Me too,' Hector said, reaching for the gravy and pouring out a generous helping.

'You do not,' Zoe corrected him. 'You're just copying Zac.'

'Do too!' he said defiantly, pouring more gravy. He scooped up a soggy potato with his spoon and swallowed hesitantly. He put his spoon down and stared at the plate sadly.

'Told you,' Zoe said, helping him scrape some of the gravy off.

The adults chattered away, laughing over the clinking of forks and knives on plates. Then Evie's stomach turned for a second time when she caught what her mum was saying.

'So, Evie has been spending time with a new friend from school – Sarah?'

Evie went still and listened.

'Sarah . . .' Ms Underhill repeated, thinking. 'I can't think of a Sarah in their year. Evie,' she said, turning around in her seat, 'what's Sarah's surname?'

Evie panicked. She hadn't anticipated this, and knew if she made up a surname she'd easily be found out. Ms Underhill knew the name of every student at St Mary's. In that moment, her mind raced through the possibilities – saying 'I don't know', or using the last name of an actual Sarah at school. She made a snap decision and swiped her arm across her glass of water, knocking it over and flooding Hector's overfull plate. Watery gravy flowed everywhere. Hector screamed. Everyone else leaped up from the table and backed away.

'Evie!' Mum said sharply, getting up to find a tea towel.

'I am so sorry,' Evie said to Hector, but felt relieved as everyone scattered to get more towels or sponge their clothes. By the time they came back to the table, the conversation had moved on. She was off the hook, for now at least.

After lunch, the parents had coffee. It was fully dark now, and Hector and Zac went outside with torches to find bugs while Evie, Zoe and Bella went upstairs. Evie was happy to be away from the adults, and tried to feel more cheerful.

'Want to plait hair?' Evie asked. She was very good at plaiting, and people were always asking her to do their hair. The others looked unsure, but Evie was determined to win them round, and got a plastic box from under her bed. She popped open the top, revealing a pile of colourful hair bands and pins.

'Bella, how about I do you one that goes around your

head like a crown?' Evie said. Bella softened and shuffled in front of Evie. Evie took a big brush out of her vanity and carefully brushed Bella's wavy auburn hair until it looked smooth and glossy. As she wove the plait around Bella's head, she turned to Zoe.

'Yours is too short for that, but I can pin it up.'

Zoe looked pleased. Holding the strands of hair in her fingers and swapping them over and under without losing any took Evie's mind off the near-miss at lunch. It took her whole brain to get it perfect.

When Evie was done, Bella and Zoe had their hair tucked up neatly with jewelled hair pins. Evie held up a hand mirror so each of them could admire the back, just like in a salon. The three sat quietly for a few seconds. Zoe broke the silence with a giggle.

'What is it?' Evie asked.

'I was just thinking of that gravy running all over the table.' She burst into laughter. 'You know, Hector looked so relieved that he didn't have to eat that horrible plate of food drowned in gravy!'

They all laughed. Evie could have told poor Hector to never copy Zac in anything.

'So what was that your mum was saying about someone named Sarah in our class?' Bella asked. 'We don't know a Sarah.'

Evie ran her tongue over her braces, her mind racing for a response.

'Mum got confused,' she said. 'She's not from school. I know her from netball camp.' Evie had gone to one week of netball camp last summer, and it was the only thing she'd ever done without anyone else they knew.

'What school does she go to?' Bella asked.

Evie grasped for a school where Bella was least likely to know anyone. 'Um, Bambrooke,' she said, trying not to make it sound like a question. Bambrooke was a private school the next neighbourhood over, and Evie herself didn't know anyone there, so hopefully Zoe and Bella didn't either.

'Hm,' Bella said. 'Well, you should invite her round sometime – we'd like to meet your secret friend, right, Zoe?' she said with a laugh. Zoe nodded.

Bella held up the mirror, admiring her appearance, running her fingers across the neat plait circling her head. 'I like it,' she said to Evie.

Evie wondered how long she could get away with hiding . . . whatever it was she had with Maryam. It would be worth it if they could solve the mystery. She thought with excitement about how her parents had agreed to the trip to Cambridge – she just needed to hang on for one more week.

DELHI, INDIA

1930–1931

13. Safia

Safia sat on the floor of Kathy's room, sketching. She was most interested in sketching the heavy rosewood furniture along each wall of the room, but as Kathy was leaning against her four-poster bed, she sketched her too. She worked quickly, knowing Ali and Abid would only cover for her for so long.

Kathy was a terrible subject. She found it impossible to stay still. Safia clicked her tongue.

'You must stop moving around,' she scolded.

'Pfff.' Kathy exhaled, blowing a strand of hair out of her face.

They sat with a wireless radio between them, turned down low. Safia didn't have one in her house, and loved listening to Kathy's to practise her English. She wasn't, however, allowed inside Kathy's house, so they kept the volume down, closed the door, and put a chair in front of it to give them a few seconds in case someone tried to come in. So far, Kathy's parents hadn't come looking for her and Anjali pretended not to notice.

Bandar sat with them and Kathy was feeding him grapes. He scuttled up to the top of one of her bedposts and, with a little grunt, threw a grape at Safia.

'Ow!' she protested, laughing. Bandar got jealous easily.

'I think he wants to be in the portrait,' Kathy said.

'He moves even more than you do,' Safia replied, but began sketching him next to Kathy despite him darting all around the room.

The radio went a bit fuzzy and Kathy twisted the knob ever so slightly to catch a signal. The BBC news broadcast had covered the economic collapse in America, Constantinople changing its name to Istanbul, and the first ever football World Cup that would be happening over the summer. Then the news moved to India, and Safia's ears pricked up.

'Today, Mahatma Ghandi, leader of the Indian National Congress, reached a milestone in his campaign

of civil disobedience – 240 milestones, to be exact. He has walked from Ahmadabad to the coastal Indian town of Dandi, gathering supporters along the way, to intentionally break the salt laws, which tax the production or purchase of salt. Upon arriving in Dandi yesterday, he was greeted at the seashore by a crowd of 50,000 people. Gandhi declared, "I want world sympathy in this battle of right against might." Today, he once again went to the shore, raised a handful of salty mud, and said, "With this, I am shaking the foundations of the British Empire." He then boiled it in water from the sea, thus producing illegal salt. He urged his followers to do the same. It is expected that he will be arrested imminently.'

This was the first time Safia had heard India as a leading story on the British news. The story itself was hard for her to understand. It seemed that there was a tax on salt, but it struck her as absurd that someone could be arrested for making salt from sea water.

She'd heard the adults in her *mahallah* talking about Gandhi and how he was gaining more support. One would say, 'Should we go to his protest?' and then another would say, 'But that is a Hindu movement,' and still another would say, 'Nai, he has Muslim support. As he says, we are one people.' And then, generally, no one would do anything.

Safia's own parents had sympathy for Gandhi, but mostly he made them scared for their business. Abbu said that the protestors were being foolish – that India needed British investment, and only a fool would bite the hand that fed it. Amma said that if she must choose between independence and feeding her family, she'd choose food every time.

'My father's gone there,' Kathy broke in, interrupting Safia's thoughts. 'To Dandi. To find out what the criminals are doing so the army can stop them.'

Safia stopped drawing. 'Criminals?' she responded in shock. Surely the army wasn't needed to stop a protest, especially a protest that seemed so clearly justified to her. But when she met Kathy's face, she saw a flat expression. Kathy hadn't been trying to upset her – 'criminals' was just the word she used for such people.

'You know,' Kathy went on, trying to explain, 'the people who are breaking the laws. They're doing it so intentionally, and as a big group. It's really rather menacing. They can hardly be surprised when the army comes to stop them, can they?'

Safia balled up her fists instinctively and took a deep breath. She couldn't tell what was more infuriating – what Kathy was saying or that she had a point. The people breaking the law technically *were* criminals, but it still wasn't right. Her blood thumped in her temples. It was difficult to find the words she wanted to say in English.

'The law is unfair,' was all Safia could put together. 'Do you understand . . .' she began, then stopped to consider her words. 'In Gujarat they live by the sea. They make salt. They have always made it. The British . . .' Safia looked to Kathy for help, but Kathy didn't know what she was trying to say. 'The British . . . do not own the sea. They make us pay tax to them to buy our own salt. Some people, they starve from too little salt.'

'You can starve from too little salt?' Kathy asked, puzzled.

'You can!' Safia shot back, disbelieving that Kathy didn't already know this.

'But those laws have always been there. Father says Gandhi just wants power and attention,' Kathy said. She looked down, seeming reluctant to meet Safia's eyes.

Safia comprehended English better than she could

speak it. She understood Kathy's point well enough to want to argue back, but didn't have the words to do so. 'What would you do . . .' she started, looking around Kathy's room for an example. She took a grape and clicked her tongue, inviting Bandar to approach. He came and sat in her lap. 'What would you do if I took this monkey, and said he is mine now, but you can buy him back for a very high price.'

'I'd say that's theft,' Kathy answered.

'Exactly,' Safia said.

Kathy looked down in thought. 'Well, still,' she said, 'it's Father's job to try to keep people from breaking the law. Even if the law isn't fair.'

Safia felt this was a totally insufficient response. But they seemed to be at an impasse and Safia sensed they wouldn't get any further. She sighed and took up her drawing pad again.

Kathy's hand suddenly darted over to the radio and turned it down. She looked up at Safia and pointed at her ear to signal that she'd heard someone coming. Quickly, she moved the chair from behind the door and peeked out. As she did, Safia slipped, on her belly, under the bed to hide.

After a moment, Kathy whispered, 'Come on. I hear

Mother moving around the corridor. I'll take you out the back.'

Safia got up, dusted herself off, and moved behind Kathy. She kept her body as hidden as she could as they crept quickly to the back stairwell, which led outside. Safia breathed a sigh of relief as they came out into the garden behind Kathy's home. Safia was permitted – though not very welcome – outside in the garden.

'I will go now,' Safia said.

'OK,' Kathy said. Then, linking her arm in Safia's, said, 'Please let's not fight. I'm sorry if I spoke about things I don't understand.'

'It's all right,' Safia responded. 'I am not sure I understand so much either.'

Safia walked through the iron gate, wondering about whether the world was changing or whether she was just aware of more than she used to be. As a child, she hadn't questioned things very much. The British had lots of money, and mostly lived separately from Indians, and in a way, it seemed like that was how things should be. But now she knew Kathy, and saw that she was just a girl – a girl like her rather than a different species.

And now that she was older, she could understand more of what she overheard adults talking about, and they seemed to be talking about Gandhi and Indian independence more than she'd ever noticed before.

It was April, and starting to get hot, but it was still cool enough for her to want to go for a stroll. Instead of heading back to her parents' shop, Safia wandered south, into the crowded streets of Chandni Chowk. She turned up a narrow, cobbled street lined with concrete buildings. Laundry hung off the balconies like colourful flags, flapping faintly in the weak breeze.

Safia turned right, not going anywhere in particular. A group of boys played cricket in the street and stopped bowling so she could walk by. As she passed a cream-coloured concrete building with wrought-iron bars on the windows, she heard a woman's voice, speaking loudly and with the tinny ring that comes from speaking through a megaphone. Safia couldn't tell what the woman was saying, but she spoke in rousing tones, and the crowd clapped and cheered when she paused.

Safia peered into the doorway and saw a corridor that led to a paved courtyard, which was full of women.

She went through. There were about forty women, most fanning themselves, sitting on their heels or standing, arms folded, at the back. Safia hovered at the entrance to the courtyard, not sure if she was allowed to enter.

Her eyes went to the small, wiry woman with the megaphone. She wore her hair in a low bun and a sari of simple white cotton – in a rough, homemade material called *khadi*. When she spoke, the crowd was silent, hanging on her every word. A young woman at the back handed Safia a pamphlet, printed lightly and on thin paper, which had an image of women walking hand in hand.

'My sisters, we must fight!' the woman called into the megaphone. 'No, not with guns or knives, but with economics. With *money*.' The crowd cheered. Safia wasn't sure what this meant. She had no money to speak of, and she would bet that none of the other women in the room did either.

'I ask you a question,' the woman went on. 'Why is it that we grow the cotton here in India, only to have it sent to mills in England, and then sold back to us? I will tell you: it is to make profit for the British, and to keep us poor!'

Murmurs went around the room. Someone shouted,

'Yes, Vijaya!', which must have been the woman's name. Safia realised with horror that she'd walked into a meeting about boycotting foreign cloth. Her eyes darted around, looking for any adults she recognised. Luckily, there were none. If her parents knew she was here she'd surely get in trouble. Most of the cloth they sold came from foreign mills, and this was the one boycott they would definitely never support. But she didn't want to leave – she wanted to listen.

'So we must not submit, my sisters.' Vijaya's voice was now so low it was almost a whisper. 'We must not take part in this system, which bleeds us dry and makes them rich. We must practise another principle: non-possession.'

Safia looked down at her pamphlet and saw a list of principles, but struggled to read them. This was starting to sound like a religion, like the 'Hindu stuff' Abbu had sometimes referred to.

Vijaya went on. 'Non-possession is the principle of taking only what one needs, no more and no less. We practise non-possession because owning beautiful things will not bring us happiness – they only suck away our money and give it to our oppressor.'

Safia thought about the beautiful fabrics that lined the table in front of her parents' shop, about how expensive they were to buy, to be resold to Indians who saved up to buy them for a special occasion or to the British, who had a taste for fine silks. She had never thought about the fact that the silks and cottons were grown in India. It was the same as the salt.

Safia looked down at the deep purple hue of her *salwar kameez* and shrank back a bit, feeling ashamed of how beautiful it looked. Because it was her parents' business, she had always had more colourful fabrics than others in her neighbourhood could afford. She was proud of the bright, jewelled hues she and her mother wore. This was the first time anyone had suggested she should feel otherwise.

'The only way,' Vijaya continued, her voice growing in strength, 'is *Swadeshi*. *Swadeshi* means self-sufficiency. It means keeping what we grow, right here in India!' The crowd cheered back. She built her voice into a loud, clear call that rang across the crowded courtyard and into the street. 'Why should we send the cotton from *our* fields, the silk from *our* worms, across the world to line the pockets of people who don't care if we live or die?'

The whole crowd was standing now, cheering. Safia found herself clapping along. She felt that the woman must be right, although she also felt that the beautiful colour of her *shalwar kameez* couldn't possibly be wrong.

'And the best part, sisters,' Vijaya continued once the cheering died down, 'is that there is a way to do it – a simple way.' She moved over to the back of the courtyard, just a few feet from Safia, where there was a large object under a sheet. She pulled the sheet off with a flourish to reveal a wooden spinning wheel. 'You surely will have seen Mr Gandhi with his famous spinning wheel. You will have heard him call on all of us to make our own cloth and build an industry here in India. I call on you, women of Delhi, to join him!'

The crowd of women – ranging from teenage girls to grandmothers with walking sticks – was chanting, '*kha-di, kha-di, kha-di*', the name of the rough, basic fabric they'd weave. Safia looked around the room. She had never seen them, the women of Delhi, so fearless.

Then, suddenly, Vijaya turned in Safia's direction. 'And look,' she said, turning her gaze on Safia and extending her hand. 'Isn't it beautiful to see such young ones joining the Sisters of India? The young are the future of this country!'

Safia's heart pounded as she saw all the eyes in the courtyard turn towards her. The dozens of women – from teenagers to the elderly – looked at her warmly, with hope. Safia felt only panic that she'd be recognised.

'Come,' Vijaya beckoned, 'come stand with me.' Safia froze, desperately hoping she wouldn't be made to step forward from the crowd. Seeing her hesitation, Vijaya waved her over more urgently. 'What is your name, my dear?'

Seeing no other option, Safia stepped forward. 'Safia,' she said quietly.

'Safia! A beautiful name for a beautiful girl!' Vijaya boomed through her megaphone and Safia felt her face go hot. 'Safia, my sister, I ask you: will you learn to weave?'

Safia looked around at the expectant pairs of eyes in the crowd. She wasn't being asked to boycott foreign cloth, only to learn to weave. That was a relief.

She nodded. The crowd cheered. Now they were chanting her name. 'Sa-fi-a! Sa-fi-a!' She gave a little wave and stepped back into the crowd.

The young woman who had handed her the pamphlet approached, turned it over, and pointed to an address at the back. 'Go there,' she said. 'Tuesday, after afternoon prayer.'

Safia nodded, unsure of whether she would go. She hurried back down the corridor, wanting to beat the crowd, still feeling the adrenaline of having been pulled out in front of everyone. She wandered back past the cricket players, down the next street, and back up to her neighbourhood, her mind buzzing with everything she'd taken in. If Indians started boycotting foreign cloth, would her parents' business survive? If she learned to weave, could she help them somehow?

She arrived at her parents' shop and cast her eyes over the rich colours and patterns. Everything Vijaya said made sense – if Indians were going to become self-sufficient, they would need to wear simpler things that they could make themselves. And yet, she loved the kaleidoscope of fabrics, especially the ones with shimmering metallic patterns for special occasions. They made the shop, and the people who bought them for weddings or Eid, look special. She didn't know if she wanted to give them up.

Abbu was coming back from the *chai walla*, two brass cups of steaming, milky *chai* in his hands. He walked one to Amma in the back of the shop and when she came out from behind her sewing table, Safia noticed her sapphire -coloured sari. Her chiffon scarf wound around her head and floated behind her and looked like the sea. Steam filled the space between them with the scent of cardamom.

Safia realised too late that she'd been so preoccupied, she'd forgotten to hide the pamphlet. Amma's eyes went right to it and she stepped forward and took it – gently – out of her hand. Safia pinched her fingers, but it was already gone.

Amma frowned.

'What is this?'

'Um, I – I'm not sure,' Safia stuttered. 'Someone just handed it to me.'

Amma pursed her lips and put it in the bin. It wasn't until an hour later, when Amma went to the toilet, that Safia was able to fish it out – only slightly covered in chai – and hide it in the waistband of her trousers.

14. Kathy

After she said goodbye to Safia, Kathy paced around her room restlessly, thinking about the conversation – or maybe it was an argument – she'd just had with Safia. It had shaken her, had made her confused about everything she'd assumed to be true. Shouldn't she be proud to be part of the biggest empire in the world? Wasn't it clear that laws should be followed? Either she was wrong about how she saw the world or Safia was.

And what of Father's work? He was a decent man, she was fairly sure of that. He had a strong sense of right and wrong. But what if he was mistaken? What if he was on the wrong side?

Bandar leaped from the dresser to the desk and looked up at her with shiny black eyes. Kathy pulled an orange from her pocket and handed it to him. Greedily, he peeled it expertly with his tiny hands. She opened the window to let him out so he wouldn't be seen following her back out to the garden. She walked down to the end of the corridor, then took a door to her right that led to the back garden, where she retreated to the shade of the banyan tree in the back corner. The sun was bright, but this part of the garden was always cool. Bandar had already scampered up to a branch, and Kathy aimlessly clung onto the ropes that sprang out of the tree's trunk. She knew those ropes would take root and, eventually, help the tree spread right across the garden if nothing stopped it. She grasped the rope and tested if it would take her weight, but heard it crack and Bandar scurried up to a higher branch.

She was bored. Despite not getting along with Ruth, she found herself missing her and her snooty remarks. She'd been the only other girl her age in Civil Lines.

Kathy wandered back towards the house and found her mother standing under the verandah with Mrs Stevenson, a civil servant's wife, fanning herself. They were talking in hushed tones, the way adults do when they talk about something sad but that they secretly enjoy.

'Mark my words, they're going to be out there on the coast through the summer,' Mrs Stevenson said.

'Well, it does seem to have gotten rather volatile,' Kathy's mother replied. 'All over salt! Can you imagine? Going to prison over a bit of salt. They're goading us into fighting them. Just trying to make the papers, that's all it is.'

'You can die from lack of salt,' Kathy said, almost involuntarily.

Her mother shot her a sharp look. 'Well, they'll die from making a point instead.'

Safia's words ran through Kathy's head, but she knew better than to try to explain Gandhi's argument to her mother. Instead, she asked her mother about the one thing they had in common. 'When is Father returning home?'

'Heaven knows,' her mother said with a sigh.

'Soon, dear,' Mrs Stevenson cut in. 'I'm sure it will be soon. Now, why don't you go to the kitchen and see if the cook has any scones left?' Mrs Stevenson said gently, forcing a smile onto her kind, round face, and placing a hand on Kathy's back.

Kathy knew Mrs Stevenson was trying to spare her from

any adult talk about violence. She wandered around to the back of the building and loitered by the door, which was open to release hot air. A steamy, meaty smell wafted out.

'What can I do for you, Miss Kathy?' Pooja's dewy face betrayed that she wasn't entirely happy to see the girl who was constantly asking for scones to give to her friend or her monkey.

'Are there any scones left, please?'

Pooja gestured towards a table in the corner. Kathy waded over through the thick air, wiggled the tin lid off the bin, and took out a slightly hard scone. 'Thank you,' she mumbled and walked back to the banyan tree.

Then, from her spot under the tree, she saw something strange. Kevan scraped the gate open and a young officer, Hawkins, walked through. He crossed the garden with his head lowered and approached her mother and Mrs Stevenson. He put a hand on her mother's arm and said something, handing her a letter. Then, she saw something she'd never seen before.

It was her mother, crying. She brought a handkerchief to her face. Then she rose from her chair, picked up her skirt with one hand, moved across the verandah, and dashed into the house. Kathy followed her with her eyes until she disappeared. Mrs Stevenson put her hand over her mouth and then followed her in. Kathy knew then that there was only one thing that would make her mother cry. She knew her father was dead.

She put what was left of the scone in her pocket and stood staring at the front door blankly. She wanted to go find Safia and tell her. But she thought she should go to her mother instead, even though she wasn't sure she'd be wanted.

Stop, she told herself. *You're being dramatic. You don't know anything at all about what's happened.* But as she watched Hawkins plod back across the lawn, she struggled to think of another explanation.

Kathy wondered why she wasn't crying. She drifted out to the verandah where her mother and Mrs Stevenson had been sitting, sat in a wicker chair, and mindlessly crumbled the scone in her pocket with her fingers. Bandar jumped down from the windowsill above and gobbled up the crumbs that spilled to the floor. Kathy stayed there, waiting for someone to confirm what she was sure was the truth.

*

The days after her father's death were a blur. Kathy's mother had Anjali dye the new white dress – the one with the mango stain – black, and she retreated to her room, closing the shutters and staying on her own all day. The officers and soldiers in her father's regiment and their wives came by to express their condolences and to bring food or flowers. Their sitting room filled with lilies, which Anjali put in jugs and topped up with water, but Kathy's mother insisted on the shutters staying closed and they soon began to wilt. They filled the room with a sickening scent that Kathy couldn't bear, and so she spent those days outside, trailing behind Anjali as she did her work, or wandering around Safia's neighbourhood, helping her run errands for her parents.

She now sat in a rocking chair on the verandah, watching the rain, which dumped down in straight sheets, driving everyone inside. She thought of Safia's parents' market stall. They would have pulled their table in and tied down the awning until it passed. Mrs Stevenson approached along the verandah, taking the rocking chair next to her and sitting with a needlepoint pattern in her lap. Mrs Stevenson had started coming round almost every day since Father died.

'How are you keeping, dear?' she said, her eyes wrinkled with concern.

'I'm fine, thank you,' Kathy said. She was being polite, but she also wasn't sure what the honest answer to this question was. In the week since her father had died, she'd felt numb. She knew she was meant to feel overwhelming sadness, like her mother seemed to, but she felt nothing. She'd hardly cried at all. The truth was, her father wasn't around very much under normal circumstances, and when he did make an appearance – for breakfast, or Sunday lunch – their relationship was formal. He would quiz her on geography or correct her use of cutlery. She knew that somewhere, deep inside, she did love him, but she couldn't seem to tap into that feeling just now, no matter how she tried.

'I've brought you something to keep you busy,' Mrs Stevenson said, handing her the needlepoint. It had a pattern of a bouquet of flowers on it. Kathy hated needle-point, but she took it and thanked her mother's friend.

Mrs Stevenson stayed in the chair, looking at her with sympathy, as if expecting Kathy to say something. But Kathy wasn't sure what to say, so she just stared out at the rain. Mrs Stevenson filled the silence.

'I know it must be a terribly hard time for you,' she said. 'But things will get easier when you move back home.'

Kathy's head snapped from the rain to Mrs Stevenson. Her throat felt like it was closing in on itself. She could just about croak out, 'Home?'

'Yes, dear, to Britain,' she said, sounding caught off guard. 'Oh my, I thought your mother would have told you. I shouldn't have said anything, but I suppose you'd have found out sooner or later . . .' She looked over her shoulder anxiously. 'Things will be easier for you and your mother there. This is no place for a child. You need a proper school and your own people.'

Kathy felt paralysed, not knowing where to begin in her panic. *My own people?* she thought, her mind racing. How could people she'd never met be her own people? Safia and her family, Anjali, Pooja, and Mrs Stevenson – *those* were her people. Britain was just an imaginary place that the adults spoke of like it was a magical land. They thought everything was better there. They longed to return. But to Kathy, it was just a foreign country where she knew no one. For the first time that week, tears – real tears – filled her eyes and spilled over onto her cheeks.

'There, there,' Mrs Stevenson said, reaching her plump hand over to stroke Kathy's wrist. 'Let it all out.'

'I need some time alone, please,' Kathy gasped. She rose from her chair, paced across the lawn and nodded at Kevan to open the gate. Once she was out, she broke into a jog down the tree-lined street, past the park, and into Kashmiri Gate.

The rain had driven most into their homes or shops, and the streets were nearly empty. Kathy's feet felt wet in her shoes and her muslin dress was soaked through. She reached her hand up to wipe the tears away – her hand and cheek were both dripping.

She walked around Safia's parents' closed shop and to the gate leading onto the courtyard in the back.

'Safia!' she shouted, peering through the bars.

Safia's grandmother was stirring a tub of laundry under the roof of the porch and looked up with a combination of alarm and annoyance. She clicked her tongue and said something in Urdu as she pulled a thin towel – more like a rough sheet – from the washing line, opened the gate, and handed it to Kathy. Safia's mother came out of the flat and must have thought Kathy was still overcome by her father's death. She pulled Kathy in under the roof, went back in and came out with Safia, who knew there must be something else.

'What's happened?' she asked Kathy.

Kathy wiped her face with the towel. 'We're going back,' she said. She ground her foot into the damp dirt floor. 'Soon.'

15. Safia

Safia stood over the steaming pot, gasping for air in the heat. The smell of the frying spices and the smoke of the coal were suffocating. Amma seemed immune to the heat or the burning feeling Safia had in her eyes, and looked down at the pot as she stirred.

'Remember that you must keep the spices moving so they don't burn,' Amma said, seeing that Safia's attention was elsewhere.

Safia nodded as she looked out the window in the back of the house, where their small kitchen, and all those near them, sent cooking smells into the courtyard. Ali gave her a wave as he climbed on his bike, a woven bag slung across his chest. He was off to his job as a courier, delivering letters and packages across Delhi.

'Why can't I go out like Ali?' Safia asked. She knew the answer to this, but she asked anyway because she didn't find the answer satisfying.

'You must learn how to run a house, Safia,' said Amma, not for the first time, 'and Ali must learn how to earn a living. Soon he will be married, and will start a family of his own.'

Ali was promised to Zainab, a beautiful, round-faced girl from the *mahallah* who he'd known and loved most of his life. Ali was the eldest, the most athletic, the best-looking, the most charming. Despite their family not having much, he was able to command a decent dowry. Everyone should have hated him, but he was so confident and outgoing that you couldn't help but cheer him on. Safia wondered how their middle brother Abid, who was shy and awkward, would fare. He refused to entertain the idea of marriage, burying himself in a book in his corner of the flat.

Safia felt like she'd aged a decade in the two weeks since she'd turned twelve. Kathy was leaving for England – today was her last day – and Safia could already feel a sense of adventure draining from her life. She was meeting Kathy today to say goodbye, and she dreaded it.

191

In this same period, Amma had begun dragging her into the adult world. She'd suddenly realised that Safia lacked all sorts of cooking and cleaning skills, although she was impressed with how quickly she'd picked up sewing. Safia didn't tell her that she'd been to a spinning lesson the previous Tuesday.

'You'll be starting a family of your own before long too,' Amma said, as if stepping into her train of thought. 'It will come sooner than you think.' She handed Safia the wooden spoon to keep the spices moving while she prepared to add the meat. It plopped in the pot with a sizzle. 'Hafsa Auntie mentioned that they are getting ready to find a match for Jamal and would like to come round for tea.'

Hafsa was a stern, pious woman – technically a cousin – who taught Quran lessons, and her son Jamal was Safia's age, holier-than-thou, and humourless. He once saw Safia feeding a stray dog and said that true Muslims only like cats, which was when she knew he was completely tedious. Safia understood that Hafsa's comment was a hint – that she was testing whether Safia might be such a match for Jamal. It was a subject their parents had been hinting at for years.

It would be, by all accounts, a good match for her. Jamal's family was respectable and wealthier than her own – Jamal would take over his father's accountancy business when he was old enough. Yet the thought of moving into Hafsa's strict home as Jamal's wife made Safia feel like she was suffocating in the fuggish smoke of the kitchen, like she might vomit if she didn't escape.

She exhaled and stepped into the courtyard to take a deep breath in, putting her hand on the wall to steady herself. She took the lid off the earthenware pot, dipped the brass ladle into it, scooped out the cool water, and took a drink. If marrying Jamal was a possibility, then she – rationally – should try to do it. She wouldn't have much of a dowry, so she wouldn't be able to be picky. Jamal and his family were people she knew and was connected to – they were basically kind and wouldn't treat her badly. Yet, it felt completely impossible.

And if not Jamal, who knew what other impossible options may present themselves? She realised, learning against the concrete wall, her thinking cleared by a light breeze, that she had no idea who else she might eventually be betrothed to. Her parents loved her, and would try to find her a match that would make her happy, but there were practicalities to consider too.

The sip of water fortified Safia enough to go back into the hot haze of the kitchen and excuse herself. Amma had just poured a cup of liquid into the pot for the meat to stew, and everything dripped with condensation.

'Amma, I'm sorry, but I need to go see Kathy. She's leaving tomorrow,' she said, heading for the door.

'Wait,' Amma said, leaving the pot on the stove to fetch something from the table. She came back with a folded square of pink and blue fabric and handed it to Safia. 'I made her a *dupatta*. As a farewell gift.' Safia looked down at the shimmering embroidered flowers, surprised and touched that Amma had sewn something for her friend. 'Wish her a safe journey from me. Take the back alley, and make sure you're back to help make the *roti*.'

Safia covered her head and walked with purpose out the back of their building, across the courtyard, through the back gate, and down a narrow alley. This time, she decided, she'd follow instructions. She followed the back alley until she had to turn onto the main road, crossed the tram tracks, dodged a bicycle and could see Kathy at their usual meeting point in the street by the Kashmiri Gate.

She looked preoccupied, kicking stones around on the pavement, but brightened when she saw Safia approaching.

'Hello!' Her eyes immediately went to the square of fabric. 'What's that?'

'A gift,' Safia said, handing it over. 'Amma made it for you.'

Her nose twitching with glee, Kathy unfolded the scarf into its full length and admired the small flowers on the shimmering pink and blue silk. 'It's *gorgeous*, Safia.' She draped it around her neck as they began to walk their usual loop, alongside the gardens and up to Kathy's neighbourhood. 'I feel terrible that I haven't brought anything for you.'

'Don't worry,' Safia replied, but then Kathy's face lit up.

'Hang on, I do have something . . . !' She pointed to the monkey, which was perched on a wall, nibbling a lychee, probably stolen, out of its tiny hands. 'Bandar! I can't take him with me, so he can be yours now!'

'Um.' Safia looked up at the monkey. She and Bandar had never really got along and she found him mildly sinister. 'Thanks.' Bandar chucked the lychee at her. Maryam thought he'd survive on his own just fine.

They turned the corner and walked down a quieter alley.

Kathy glanced at her tarnished pocket watch. 'I only have a few minutes before I have to go. Our train leaves soon.'

'How will you get to Britain?' Safia asked.

Kathy's eyes gleamed. She had every leg of the journey memorised and took a big breath in. 'A train to Bombay, then a boat through the Red Sea to Cairo. Then across the Mediterranean, through the Strait of Gibraltar, and up the coast of Spain and France.' Her voice was breathless with excitement. 'I cannot *wait* to see Egypt! We're going to stop in Cairo for two days and I've been begging Mother to see the pyramids.'

Safia hadn't realised that Kathy was looking forward to the journey, and she felt a small pang of hurt. She thought they were agreed that there was nothing positive about Kathy leaving. But now she was getting ready to see the world while Safia was stuck in a kitchen learning how to stew lamb.

Kathy seemed to sense she had misjudged her tone and said, 'But I'm sure it won't be as special as I'm making it sound. I'd still rather not go.' She changed the subject. 'What have you been doing this morning?'

Maryam told her about the cooking lessons, and all the other domestic chores. She told her about Jamal, too.

'What?' Kathy stopped in her tracks and readjusted her scarf. 'You're still a child, Safia. Your parents can't possibly be thinking about marriage yet.'

This was how Safia felt too, but she found herself getting defensive when Kathy said it. 'Well, it would not be tomorrow. These things take time,' she came back. A marriage could take years to agree and plan. 'Besides, your mother is always talking about the qualities you will need to be a respectable woman. I believe she is talking about the qualities you will need to find a husband, no?'

Kathy considered this. 'I suppose she is,' she concluded. 'But that's also ridiculous. I don't want anything to do with polite society just yet.'

As usual, Kathy had managed to instantly diffuse any tension, and Safia found herself wanting to talk more. 'I want . . .' She paused to find the words. 'I want things to stay the same,' she said. 'I do not want you to leave. I do not want life to get so serious.'

Bandar trailed behind them, and Kathy pulled some peanuts out of her pocket and dropped them in the street for him. 'Me too,' she said.

Afternoon prayer was ending and people were coming out of the mosque. The street was growing crowded, and Kathy steered them up towards Civil Lines.

'Well, you don't *have* to get married to him, do you?' Kathy asked. 'It's your life. Surely you can say no.'

'It is not so easy,' Safia replied. 'Who else can I marry? My parents don't have much money for the dowry.'

'Oh,' Kathy replied, looking slightly stumped. 'Well, there's always bank robbery.'

Safia had to look at her to know she was joking. She would miss Kathy's refusal to take anything seriously.

Safia's chest tightened as they climbed the familiar hill of Kathy's street. She knew it was nearing the time to say goodbye as they approached the big gate. Kevan looked less stern today. Maybe he knew Kathy was leaving.

Kathy stopped at the iron gate. 'You just need someone

who you like as much as me,' she joked, 'although I know that's going to be difficult.'

Safia laughed at her lack of modesty. 'It will be boring without you here.'

'I know,' Kathy responded, squinting into Safia's face. 'I wish I could stay.'

Safia wondered if Kathy would ever return to Delhi. 'Do you think we will meet again?' she asked.

'Of course,' Kathy replied without missing a beat. 'I'll be back just as soon as I can. And anyhow, you'll come to London when you're a famous artist.' Safia snorted but Kathy's expression was serious.

They stood like that for a moment, feeling the breeze that rustled through the trees and looking down on the streets they'd walked together hundreds of times. Then, glancing again at her pocket watch, Kathy unwound her scarf and draped it grandly over her shoulders, casting one end across herself with a dramatic flourish. She jutted her chin out imperiously.

'Well, *dahling*,' she said in an exaggerated posh accent. 'I've a train to catch.'

Safia took her by the shoulders and squeezed. 'Write

me a letter as soon as you can,' Safia said. 'I must keep practising my English, after all.'

'I promise,' Kathy said, pulling her in for a hug. 'Goodbye, Safia.' With that, she turned on her heel and marched to the gate, waving the shining strip of pink and blue fabric at Safia.

Safia turned and walked down the hill. Her heart was hurting, and though she knew it was harder for Kathy than it was for her, she still wasn't sure what she was going to do with herself tomorrow, or the day after that.

Her shadow was getting long on the pavement – it was nearly time to make the *roti*, but she wasn't ready to go home yet. Making her way back into the snaking alleys of brightly coloured concrete, she felt in her pocket for a coin. She would, she thought, pay Naeem a visit to bring him a gift for his pigeons.

LONDON, UK

PRESENT DAY

16. A Day Trip

Maryam tore off a piece of flaky *paratha*, which smelled buttery and felt warm, and used it to scoop up the gravy of the *nalli nihari* in front of her, which was rich and brown, with bits of lamb in it. The kids at school would surely look at the bowl of lamb stew with a big bone sticking out of it and think it was awful, but it was so delicious that, for a minute, she focused on nothing else.

But really, her mind was elsewhere. Mum had gone to the landlord's office to try to discuss their rent in person. She had told Dad that he should stay home – he lost his temper too easily and would probably end up storming out.

Dad looked anxiously at his watch and the buzzing anxiety returned to her stomach and spread through her limbs.

'She should be back soon,' he said. Maryam, Nani and Hassan each nodded but didn't have much else to add. Unable to wait any longer, Dad went back to the shop without finishing his food, taking the radio with him so he could keep listening to the cricket.

Shortly after Dad left, Maryam heard the key turn in the lock. No one shouted down the corridor to Mum – they waited on the edge of the sofa as she came in and sat down in the chair by the TV. She took her hijab off and sat there silently for a moment, either not aware of the tension in the room or not ready to respond to it. Her eye make-up had smudged and it made her look weary.

'The rent is going up,' she said at last, to no one in particular. 'Next month.' She looked down at her hands and Maryam could see her breathing deeply. Nani pressed herself up with her walking stick and went over to Mum's chair. As if her presence unlocked something, Mum rested her head on Nani's stomach and sobbed. Maryam had never seen either of her parents cry, and looked away, feeling like she shouldn't see it. Hassan must have felt the same because he retreated to their room. Maryam suddenly got the feeling that this was bad – really bad.

Nani stroked Mum's hair, saying something in Urdu. Something about God.

Then, as if remembering herself, Mum pulled away, took a deep breath, and wiped her eyes. She reached out and rubbed Maryam's leg. 'I don't mean to scare you, Mari. It will be OK,' she said. 'I just needed to let that out.'

But Maryam felt unconvinced. She wasn't little any more – she needed to understand what was happening. Wordlessly, she got up and went to her room. Her mum followed her with her gaze but Nani whispered, 'Let her go.'

Maryam pushed the door open hesitantly. Hassan was lying on the bottom bunk, staring at the wooden slats above him. Maryam sat on the floor.

'Mum said the rent is going up *next month*,' she said, although she knew he'd heard that part. He kept looking up, throwing a foam ball against the slats above him. 'Why is this happening?' She knew Hassan would tell it to her straight. Not tell her some rubbish about how it would be OK or this was God's plan or something.

Hassan was silent for a few seconds, then turned to

look at her. His expression was shaken and afraid. But after a beat he regained the appearance of calm. 'Do you know what gentrification is?'

'Yeah,' Maryam answered automatically, but when Hassan raised his eyebrows, she corrected herself. 'Actually, no. But I don't want one of your political lectures, Hassan. I just want to know what's going to happen.'

He looked back up and started throwing the ball again. 'I don't know what's going to happen. But you asked *why*.'

Maryam closed her mouth and pushed her glasses up the bridge of her nose to show she was listening.

'You know how everything has been getting posher around here?' Maryam nodded. She knew what he meant: little shops on the high street popping up one by one – all-white coffee bars, boutiques that sold beautiful hardcover books and candles. She had never gone into any of them. 'Well, the landlord decided he can actually make a lot more money letting to one of those places, and he's raising the rent.'

'But he can't just do that, can he?' Maryam was out-raged. Surely you couldn't just change the rent on someone whenever you wanted.

'Well, it looks like he probably can,' Hassan said. She hadn't noticed him grab their mum's phone on the way to the bedroom, but she saw now that he'd been looking up the law on Citizens Advice. 'It says here that if other rents in the area have gone up, and if he's given notice, then he can.'

Maryam slumped in her spot. Everyone was talking about it as if the rise in rent was final, but there *must* be something they could do.

'How much is he raising it by?' she asked.

'I don't even know, man, but I think . . . a lot.'

'Maybe we should try to raise the money. It *could* work, right?' Maryam had heard stories of people raising money online to save local businesses or get treatment for their sick kid.

'Look, I don't mean to crush your dreams,' he said, 'but I'm not sure the people with money to donate want to save a random corner shop.'

Maryam breathed out hard. She knew he was right.

'So what's going to happen?' she asked.

For the first time Maryam could remember in her life, her big brother didn't have an answer. Looking back up at the wooden slats, he shrugged. 'Genuinely, Mari, I don't know.'

Judging from her mum crying into Nani's dressing gown, Maryam knew she didn't either, and that made her feel so afraid it was like someone was sitting on her chest, stopping her from focusing on anything else until the pressure went away.

She felt grateful for the trip to Cambridge the next morning to distract her. It would get her away from the stress and gloom of her flat – if only for a day.

Maryam woke up earlier than usual, nervous for the journey. She chose what she thought were her nicest looking casual clothes: jeans (the right length, and no holes) and a fluffy pink jumper. She brushed her hair and put it in a long, neat plait. She hoped she looked like the kind of friend you'd want to bring on a family trip.

She told herself she was Sarah, imagining herself responding to different people calling her Sarah. She felt like a spy, taking on a false identity and going on a secret mission.

'Big day, Sarah,' Hassan said, walking into their room

with a piece of toast. He'd been calling her Sarah since the previous night to get her used to it.

Maryam packed a backpack with the notebook, her Oyster card, a water bottle and a pen. She wondered aloud if she needed to bring anything else.

Hassan shrugged. 'Fake ID?' he joked.

She put on her coat and backpack, but didn't rush her mum. The later they were, the less time the parents would have to chat. She prepared responses to getting caught in the lie in her head, but nothing sounded convincing.

But soon enough, they were walking out the door. The sky was clear and a thin frost crunched under their feet in the estate courtyard, their breath making little clouds in front of them. Maryam felt so nervous she found it hard to act normal.

'So, are you looking forward to this trip?' Mum asked.

'Yup! I think it's going to be really fun,' Maryam said. She could hear the tremble in her own voice. They turned down the high street and headed towards the tube, walking in silence.

'You're thinking about the shop, aren't you?' Mum asked.

For a moment, Maryam didn't realise what she meant, then felt guilty that she actually *wasn't* thinking about the shop. 'Yeah,' she lied.

'It will be OK,' Mum said, repeating that same phrase Maryam hated. It was a lie: she didn't know it would be OK. 'We'll figure something out.'

As they approached the tube station, her palms started sweating inside her gloves, and her heart began pounding more forcefully in her chest.

A brass band was unpacking in the square outside the station, in front of the big Christmas tree. Maryam saw Evie and her parents waiting by the entrance and waved.

As they approached, she said to Mum, 'We're running late, so we don't have a lot of time to chat.'

'Don't rush me,' Mum said, looking at her watch. 'You'll be fine for your train.'

Evie looked nervous too. She was staring at the ground, pacing around. Her dad strode towards them, with his hand extended.

'Hi, I'm Mark, Evie's dad,' he said, shaking Mum's hand. 'Hi there,' he said to Maryam. Maryam was terrified he'd follow it up with 'Sarah', but he didn't.

'Hi, I'm Rezia,' Mum said. 'Thank you for this trip. We've never been to Cambridge.' It was another lucky break that her name wasn't mentioned.

'Oh, it's our pleasure,' Evie's mum responded. 'It will be nice for the girls to learn about each other's families.'

'Well, I must pay you for the train ticket,' Mum said, fumbling with her purse. 'How much do I owe you?'

'Don't worry, it wasn't much at all,' Evie's mum said, waving the purse away.

'OK, well we'd better get on our way!' Evie said briskly, looking at her watch.

Maryam's mum gave her a big hug and pressed a five-pound note into her hand. She said, 'Don't let her parents pay for anything else. And be careful, Mari.' But they were a bit too far from Evie's parents for them to hear clearly.

'I will! Bye!' Maryam said, chasing after Evie as she descended the stairs to the tube.

When they got off at Kings Cross, Maryam followed the family, who all seemed to know where they were going – even Zac. Evie slowed down to fall into step with her.

'That was lucky, huh?' she said in a low voice, smiling.

'Seriously. There were about four times when I thought someone would surely say my name,' Maryam replied.

They stepped onto an escalator into a big hall, with shops everywhere and giant screens on the wall with dozens of destinations. Maryam hadn't heard of most of the places.

'Platform four!' Zac shouted, and suddenly the family turned as one and started jogging towards the platform. Maryam ran to keep up, amazed that even the six-year-old was better-travelled than she was.

They hurried down the platform, to the very back of the train, climbed on, and claimed two tables, panting.

Soon, they were pulling away. It was Maryam's first time on a proper train – one that wasn't a tube or overground – and it felt old-fashioned and magical. Riding in a backwards-facing seat, she rested her head on the cold window. The tunnel gave way to a view of the London skyline, the Shard in the distance. Soon there were graffiti-covered walls and brick blocks of flats, and then, as they left the city, trees. Quite quickly it didn't feel like they were anywhere near London. Farmland, carved into patches, spread out on either side.

A ticket collector came down the aisle wearing a Santa hat. Evie's mum handed him a stack of tickets. The man scrutinised Evie and Maryam.

'You girls under fifteen?' he asked. No one ever thought Maryam was *older* than her age, and she nodded back, stunned.

'Yes,' Evie's mum cut in, 'they have their Oyster cards if you'd like to check.'

'Yes, please,' he said, holding his hand out. Maryam glanced anxiously at Evie. She knew her name was on the card and reluctantly dug it out of her bag. She slipped it into her palm and was careful to keep it face-down as she handed it over.

'Mm hmm,' he said and handed the stack of tickets and both cards back to Evie's mum. 'There you go, enjoy your trip.' Maryam exhaled a sigh of relief.

Evie's mum took the stack back and Maryam's chest tightened again. She chewed on her lower lip as she watched Evie's mum flip the cards over to see whose was whose, giving Evie's back to her first. She paused on Maryam's, looking puzzled. Maryam's heart raced, trying to think of an explanation for what she knew Evie's mum

213

was seeing. Evie's mum looked across the table, meeting Maryam's eyes.

'This card says "Maryam Ahmed",' she said, holding Maryam's gaze. Maryam swallowed and looked to Evie for help.

'Sarah is what she goes by at school,' Evie cut in, but her mum raised a hand, signalling for her to stop. The game was up.

'Now, I think we both know that if I called your parents and asked them if your name was Sarah, they'd say no,' Evie's mum said, sounding like she was trying to control her anger. 'Am I wrong?'

Maryam looked down at the table and shook her head. Her glasses slid to the end of her nose and she pushed them up. She wondered what would happen now.

'OK. So I suggest you two tell me what's going on. And this time, I'd like the truth,' Evie's mum said. By this time, her dad and Zac had given up trying to look like they weren't listening and leaned across the aisle.

Maryam was silent. She wasn't sure where to start.

'Please let me explain,' Evie pleaded. Her mum turned in her seat, one eyebrow raised.

'All right then,' she said to Evie. Maryam could tell that Evie was also unsure what her explanation would be.

'Maryam and I have been working on this project together, and sort of becoming . . .' she began slowly, pausing on the next word, 'friends.' 'But a lot of the other kids – *Bella*, for example – are mean to her. Like, they make fun of her and stuff.'

Evie paused and avoided Maryam's eyes, and Maryam realised there must be all sorts of jokes about her that Evie was too embarrassed to recount with her there. It was nothing Maryam didn't already suspect, though it stung to hear it said aloud. She gave Evie a little nod to show she could go on.

'But they made *Maryam* sound like a bully,' she continued. 'You've heard how Ms Underhill talks about her. There's no way you and Dad would have let me go to her house after everything you'd heard.'

Evie's mum and dad looked at each other in sad surprise. Her mum was silent for a few moments, then sighed heavily. She reached her hand across the table and took Maryam's. Maryam instinctively drew back, not expecting this and feeling self-conscious that her palms were sweaty, but she could see that Evie's mum meant this as a kind and meaningful gesture. So, she let her hand sit limply in Evie's mum's.

'I am so sorry that you felt like you needed to pretend to be someone else. It's unfair that you were ever put in that position.' Evie's mum looked like she might cry. Maryam broke her gaze and looked away, not quite sure what to do. 'If Evie likes you, that's enough for us.'

Despite feeling uncomfortable, Maryam was relieved. They had underestimated Evie's parents, and she wished they had just told the truth from the start. She looked across the table at Evie and could tell she was thinking the same. After a polite pause, Maryam slowly crept her hand back into her own lap.

Maryam wondered if they should go a step further and tell Evie's parents about the folders and what they'd learned so far. She wished she could speak to Evie at that moment, but it wasn't right to reveal anything without Evie agreeing to it first. It was hard to even catch Evie's eye – she kept picking up her phone, glancing at it, and then putting it down. Maryam wondered if she'd told her friends where she was going, and with whom. She started to imagine Bella making fun of her on text, but stopped her mind from going there.

In Cambridge, they piled into a black cab. It was Maryam's first time, and she folded down one of the backwards-facing seats and gazed out the window at bakeries and bookshops, empty save a few students who hadn't gone home for Christmas. Then the streets became more residential, and the taxi stopped in front of a semi-detached brick house.

Evie's dad paid the fare (which was enough for at least twenty packets of crisps) and Maryam lingered behind the others, suddenly nervous about what she had come to do. What did they actually think they were going to learn by having lunch with this old woman? They couldn't exactly search the house.

Evie's mum banged the large brass knocker loudly. They heard slow movements and then a series of clicks as Evie's grandma unlocked the door.

When the door swung open, there stood a tall but hunched woman with short white hair and gold-rimmed glasses. She wore navy trousers and a chunky cardigan.

She gave a little nod and immediately turned around and shuffled back down the corridor.

'Do come in,' she called back to all of them in a tone that sounded more like an order than an invitation.

17. Gobbledygook

Gran's blue eyes had a foggy look when she met them, and she was slower and more hunched than the last time Evie had seen her. You didn't notice things like that in a video call.

Mum took Gran by the elbow and said loudly, 'Mum, this is Evie's friend, Sa—', then, catching herself, 'Maryam.'

Gran looked back to glance at Maryam, giving her a nod. 'Hello,' she said, before turning around to continue hobbling to the kitchen.

'Cuppa tea?' she asked the group as she walked straight to the kettle.

'Sure, I'll make it, Sue. You sit down,' Dad said.

'I'm not so old that I can't make a cup of tea,' Gran snapped. Dad sat at the table sheepishly. Evie winced, sneaking a glance at Maryam, who looked like a deer in headlights.

They sat in silence for a moment, listening to the whoosh of the kettle and the tinkling of spoons in tea-cups. Evie was starving and took a digestive from the tin on the table, but found it to be stale and spongy and left it half-eaten on her plate. Gran pulled out a chair, tucked herself under the table and stared blankly at her tea.

'How are you, Mum?' Mum asked.

The old woman seemed annoyed at the question. 'Oh, you know, there's nothing much for me to share. My days all blur into one another now.'

Evie was a little shaken by how much older Gran seemed than the last time she had seen her. She was even grumpier than usual, and Evie wondered what Maryam – who finished her stale biscuit with a pained look – must be thinking.

Evie checked her phone. There wasn't anything new in the 3 Amigos chat she had with Zoe and Bella beyond the messages she'd seen on the train.

Zoe: My mum said she saw your family on the tube really early this morning with a girl she didn't know. Who was it? The mysterious *Sarah*????

Bella: Oooh we need to meet her!

Evie felt like she couldn't get enough air. She'd been contemplating how to respond on the trip here, and was more confused than ever now that she didn't have to keep up the Sarah lie for her parents. There was nothing to do but deny it.

Evie: Odd. We were on the tube, but there wasn't anyone else with us.

Mum shot her a pointed look and she put the phone away.

Trying again, Mum said, sipping her tea, 'Evie and Maryam are researching each other's families for a school project. I think they'd like your help with it.'

Gran grunted and said, 'Well, OK. Didn't we talk about this already?'

Evie was starting to feel it was unlikely that they were going to get any stories at all out of her.

'Yes, but we're meant to ask you some follow-up questions too,' Evie said.

'Well, I'm not sure I'll be much use. I can't seem to remember much these days,' Gran said gruffly.

'I'm sure that's not true, Gran,' Evie said.

Her grandmother looked at her as if noticing her for the first time and smiled faintly.

'If you'd like,' she said more gently, 'but I can't promise anything interesting.'

Zac sighed loudly, his patience reaching its limit. His parents began to reprimand him, but Gran seemed to have softened slightly. Evie couldn't understand what had changed her mood. Maybe it was just feeling like someone actually did want to hear what she had to say.

'Zachary, my boy, how would you like to go to the study and have a play with your grandpa's old trains?'

Zac's face lit up and he nodded vigorously, bouncing out of his chair and grabbing Dad's arm. Dad also seemed keen to extract himself from the kitchen table, and followed Zac upstairs.

Evie took a folded piece of paper out of her bag. 'Here's the family tree we did based on what you told me,' she said, unfolding it. 'And your mother was born in Delhi, right?' She pointed to Katherine's name on the page.

'That's correct,' Gran said. 'Her father was in the army, but he died in some sort of riot. So then she moved here.

Never quite got over the weather, or the people she left back in India.'

It was amazing how Gran transformed when she spoke about the past. Evie looked at Maryam, wondering if Safia could have been one of the people who Katherine left. Maryam met her eyes. Evie could tell she was thinking the same.

'And my father was in the army too, you know,' Gran continued, sitting up a little straighter in her seat. Then, eyeing the notes Evie was taking, she added, 'He was a captain in the Suffolk Regiment. Intelligence officer.'

Evie had heard this before but still wrote it down out of politeness. Stories about her Grandpa Gordon were part of family folklore. He'd marched in every Remembrance Sunday parade, wearing his star-shaped medal, until he died. But she knew nothing about his wife, Katherine.

'Intelligence officer?' Maryam asked. 'Like, a spy?'

Gran turned her attention to Maryam, keen to tell the story to a new audience.

'I suppose it was a bit like being a spy, yes,' she said. 'He had good French and German, so he could get information from people.' Evie wondered if this was a new clue – perhaps her intelligence officer great-grandfather had something to do with the code. But something told her to stay focused on Katherine.

'So what did your mother do during the war?' Evie asked.

'Well,' Gran thought for a moment, 'I'm not sure. I imagine she would have supported the war effort, like most women. You know, coming up with recipes that used rationed ingredients, mending clothes, that sort of thing.'

At the word 'recipes', Evie stole a glance at Maryam, who raised her eyebrows in return.

Gran carried on. 'But then the war ended, and my father came home, and my mother had me shortly after.'

'What was she like?' Evie pressed.

Gran thought for a moment. 'She was a maths teacher. Mind you, most mothers didn't have jobs in those days, so she was unusual in that way. She was a kind person. Very warm. Her own mother – my grandmother – had been a terrifying woman. I don't think she wanted to be like that.' Gran took a sip of tea. Her foggy blue eyes looked far away.

Evie, who found Gran slightly terrifying, wondered if it skipped a generation.

'You know, I don't think she ever quite got over leaving India. She was always talking about going back one day to visit a friend she made there, but she never did,' Gran said.

'Why not?' Evie asked, her ears pricking up.

'It was a different time. A woman didn't just go travelling halfway around the world on her own, and India wasn't a place you'd take children on holiday. But that part of her life stayed with her for the rest of her days,' she said with a sigh. 'She always talked about someone named Safia.'

Evie looked up at Maryam with wide eyes, and Maryam looked back with her mouth hanging open. Evie had suspected their great-grandmothers had known each other, but until that moment she hadn't fully believed it. It seemed easier to imagine that she was connected to nearly any random person on Earth than to Maryam, who, despite being from her neighbourhood, seemed to be from a different world.

But all Evie said was, 'Did you say *Safia*?'

'Yes,' Gran replied, 'but it wasn't like today. You couldn't just find them on the Facebook or whatever your generation uses.'

Evie was squinting at Maryam as if seeing her for the first time. Maryam, however, was staring at Gran with an eager expression, as if she was in class and wanted to be called on. She kept drawing in breath to speak but then stopping herself.

'What has come over you two? Are you all right?' Gran asked, looking at Mum, who tried to catch Evie's eye.

'Yes, it's just . . .' Evie paused, not sure what to start with. She figured she might as well start explaining. 'Maryam's great-grandmother was named Safia, and she lived in Delhi when she was young.' She delivered this news expecting Gran to be shocked, perhaps to spit out her tea.

But Gran just said, dismissively, 'Well, it was a massive city, even then. And I think Safia is a very common name, isn't it?' She looked at Maryam as she asked this, who shrugged.

Evie was convinced of the connection now, no matter how many Safias there were in Delhi, and she needed Gran to see that something remarkable was happening.

'It's not just that,' she said quickly, reaching into her backpack and taking out her folder. 'We found these.' She put the faded red folder on the table, its *Family Recipes* label face-up. She nodded at Maryam to signal that she should do the same.

Gran's gaze glided over the folders without interest, and then she looked again, this time more closely. She took the folder from in front of Evie and opened it.

'We always had red folders like this around the house,' she said. 'I haven't seen one in a long time.'

'Wait, is that the one you showed me a couple of weeks ago?' Mum asked, looking from Evie's folder to Maryam's.

'Yup,' Evie said with satisfaction, hoping Mum now saw that there *was* something strange and interesting about the letters in the folder. 'Maryam found this one in her grandmother's things, and *get this*: the writing on her cover means "Family Recipes" in Urdu.'

Mum and Gran frowned at each other in puzzlement. 'And your great-grandmother was also born in Delhi?' Mum asked Maryam, struggling to keep up.

'*Yes*,' Evie said impatiently.

227

'But if our families are actually connected, that's really incredible.' Mum opened the cover to Evie's folder.

'Yes,' Evie said. 'It *is*.' She couldn't help wanting to make Mum sorry for ignoring the folder in the first place.

Gran went over to the kettle, flipped it on again, then walked around to Maryam, looking at her folder over her shoulder.

'What's inside?' she asked.

Evie and Maryam each opened their folders and pulled out a sheet. Mum and Gran inspected one each and then swapped. Evie and Maryam edged to the end of their seats, looking from one woman to the other, waiting for one of them to come up with an explanation.

'Do you know what they mean?' Evie finally asked.

'No. It's gobbledygook,' Gran replied. 'I haven't the foggiest idea. But this one is definitely in my mother's handwriting.' She held up the page that had come from Maryam's folder. She then thumbed through the rest of the pages. 'In fact, everything in this folder is written by her. I can say that for sure. What on earth were Mother's letters doing in your house?'

'I don't know.' Maryam sounded defensive.

228

So they *were* letters, seemingly written from Katherine to Safia. That meant the other ones must be from Safia to Katherine. But what did they say? Why not just write them in plain English?

'But why are they written like this?' Gran asked, echoing Evie's thoughts. 'It looks like some kind of code to me.'

'I don't understand,' Mum said. 'Why would Grandma need to write in code? And how did she know Maryam's great-grandmother? And why did they both have these folders?'

'That's why we're here!' Evie said. 'We came to try to figure it out.'

Mum's eyes moved to Gran, who had put down her cup of tea on the counter and was climbing the stairs, one trembling hand on the bannister, pulling herself up. She paused and looked at the others with impatience. 'Come along, will you?' she said.

Evie, her mum, and Maryam scrambled out of their chairs and followed Gran up one flight of stairs, then another to the attic. Gran pushed hard on the old wooden door, which swung open into a dark, musty room, full of old books and half-broken things. Evie had been coming up to this attic her whole life, hunting for treasures like old toys or photographs. She and Zac had always ignored the big bookshelves against the wall, with books and magazines stacked haphazardly. But this was where her gran now went directly, past rows of maths textbooks and sheet music, stepping on an old, padded footstool to reach the top shelf. Evie's mum made sounds of caution, which Gran ignored as she extended her arm and swatted at a hat box until it edged part way off so she could grab it.

'Aha,' she said breathlessly, stepping off the footstool and then sitting down on it, setting the round, striped hat box in front of her on the wooden floor. The lid was caked with dust, but Gran didn't bother to wipe it before prying it open. It was the Gran Evie knew – in charge, on a mission.

Maryam stood slightly behind Evie, looking around curiously, but followed Evie's lead when she knelt on the floor by the box. Inside was a bundle wrapped in a moth-eaten pink and blue scarf with little flowers embroidered on it. Gran unwrapped the scarf, and inside that was a pile of letters bound with twine. Evie looked up at Gran for an explanation.

'These are some letters my mother kept. I found them after she died, but never felt right reading them. I believe they are from the Safia we've been talking about.' She turned to Maryam, adding, 'Your great-grandmother.'

Evie stared at the contents of the box, hardly able to fathom that Gran actually had more of Safia's letters. But here they were, lurking in a corner of the attic that she'd never bothered to give a second glance. Evie looked down, not sure if she was allowed to take anything out.

'Go on,' Gran said. 'There's a lot to get through, so you'd better get going!'

She was making her way out the door, more slowly than she'd come into it. Mum stayed in the doorway, watching Evie intently as she spread the letters on the floor in front of her.

'Come on, Helen, let's leave them to it,' Gran ordered. Mum lingered in the doorway, seemingly wanting to stay, but Gran grabbed her arm and steered her out of the room.

Evie put herself in the mindset of a detective. Learning a lesson from Maryam's brother, she first glanced at the dates and arranged the letters in chronological order, starting in 1932 and going up to 1940. They were all from Safia, and definitely the same straight, pointy handwriting as the letters in her own folder.

'So, we know for sure now,' she said to Maryam. 'The letters in our red folders are between Safia and Katherine.' Part of Evie had assumed that her imagination was running away again. It was bewildering that what she'd suspected was *actually* true – that she and Maryam were connected through women who were friends nearly a century ago. Here were their actual letters, sitting on the floor of Gran's attic.

As Evie stared at the envelopes in wonder, Maryam tapped her foot and seemed keen to jump in, but reluctant to touch the letters herself.

'OK then,' Evie said, picking up the first letter from Safia. 'Let's do this.'

18. The Correspondence

Maryam gently opened the top envelope and wriggled out the brittle, yellowed paper inside. She noted with relief that this letter wasn't written in code. It was written in pencil and Maryam could see the places where Safia had corrected her writing. She could hardly believe that her great-grandmother had sealed this very envelope and sent it halfway across the world.

2 February 1932

Dear Kathy,

Thank you for your letter. I am sorry that it has taken me so long to write to you. I was feeling nervous about writing in English but I have found my courage now and done many correction. I am not sure how long it has taken this letter to reach you. Maybe it has been many weeks?

Your journey to England sounded very difficult. And I think your new school sounds very bad. The girl named Lily is very mean. Did she really put glue in your hair? You must not let them treat you like that. Unless you have changed, I'm sure you will fight back.

Do you remember our conversation before you left Delhi, about Jamal? I have taken your advice and found someone who I like as much as you (or almost as much). I have asked Naeem to marry me. He said yes and so did our parents. I am surprised that Abbu and Amma allowed this. He is even poorer than I am, but he is kind. We will be married next year.

Are you surprised? I hope that you are shocked!

Please write back soon.

Your friend,

Safia

Maryam took in the fact that her great-grandmother had actually written these words on this paper. Now that she read them, Safia seemed real. Kathy did too. She wasn't Katherine – a distant person on paper – but Kathy, a girl.

'Poor Kathy,' Maryam said. She found herself wanting to read more about the misery of school. Kathy sounded like an even bigger outcast than she was.

'I don't think schools used to take bullying very seriously,' Evie said dismissively. She moved on. 'So Safia asked your great-granddad to marry *her*?' Maryam shrugged, equally surprised. 'She sounds cool,' Evie said.

Maryam agreed, which was a perplexing thing to think about Nani's mum. They opened the next one.

15 November 1936

Dear Kathy,

How are you? The stories in your last letter gave me a laugh. I cannot imagine you going to so many tea parties to meet a husband. I am sorry it is so boring to pretend to be amused at the jokes of these young men. Has your mother finally convinced you to press your hair? Will you see this Gordon fellow again? He sounds nice.

'Gordon!' Evie yelped. 'That's Gran's dad!'

Naeem and I have taken over Amma and Abbu's shop. They are getting too old to run it, although Amma won't stay still and sews all day. But I mostly stay with Baby Faisal and do the cooking and cleaning. It is tiring, especially because I'm pregnant again. Naeem is running the business, but I don't think he has a head for it.

I wonder if this next baby will be a girl or a boy. I would like a girl, even though they are expensive. If it is a boy, we will call him Saleem. If it is a girl, we will call her Shehenaz. By the time I next write to you, God willing, we will know which.

I do miss you, and hope that you are happier now that you have left that awful school.

Your friend,

Safia

'Why does she say that girls are expensive?' Evie asked. 'Like, clothes and stuff?'

'No,' Maryam answered, glad to have some knowledge to share. 'Because a woman's family pays a dowry to her husband's family when she gets married.'

Evie nodded slowly. 'Huh.'

20 December 1938

Dear Kathy,

Congratulations on your marriage! How is life as a wife? I must admit that it is difficult for me to imagine you married, and to an army man!

I'm sorry it has been so long since my last letter. I've been busy with the two boys and our newborn Shehenaz, and things have been difficult here.

Maryam turned with wide eyes to Evie. 'Shehenaz! That's Nani!'

Shehenaz has been unwell, and cholera has broken out in Kashmiri Gate. I was so scared for her, but she seems to be recovering. I am thankful for that, but life has gotten very hard, Kathy. Everything is expensive. Rice costs five times as much as it did last year, and everything is in short supply. We can hardly feed ourselves. So much food is being used for the British war effort that there is not enough for the rest of us.

Cotton is also being used for the war, which means that the cloth we sell is getting more expensive to buy. It feels like we are getting poorer all the time. The British declared that India is at war too. But I do not think that anyone asked us!

Some of the British are leaving – many of Amma's old customers have gone back to Britain. It seems they now think Delhi is a dangerous place. But, more people also come here every day, to work in the factories that supply the army. People are packed into buildings, and the streets are overflowing. Everything must go to the war. The war has created jobs here, but not very good ones.

Ali has volunteered to join the army. I can hardly believe it – Ali in the British Army! I am sure that you will be as surprised as I was. I tried to talk him out of it, but his mind was made up. He said he was promised a good job after the war was over. He also mentioned the poster he saw, saying he would get to see the world. You know how impulsive Ali can be. I begged him not to do it, but he will not listen.

Naeem said maybe he should join too. The army would pay him, and we're not making much money from the shop. We can't go on like this much longer. But I still forbade him to do it. I cannot raise our children as a widow. Maybe it is

time to give up the shop – Naeem could work in a factory.
There must be another way – I just haven't thought of it yet.
Please write soon. I hope you are well.
Your friend,
Safia

Evie and Maryam sat and stared at the page for a moment. Maryam thought of little Nani, and how uncertain things were for their family. She wondered if it made Nani sad that her family was back in a position where they didn't know how to make ends meet from one month to the next.

'But it turned out OK!' Evie said to Maryam reassuringly, misreading the concern in her face. 'Your grandmother is alive, and she made it here.'

'Yeah.' Maryam wondered if things were going to get worse before they got better.

14 February 1940

Dear Kathy,
The money you sent has arrived, and it is too generous. I
hope you did not think, when I told you of the problems here,

239

that I was asking for money. But I will accept it gratefully. It makes a very big difference to us.

I must start with the sad news. Ali has died in Libya. I cannot believe it. My eldest brother, gone. He was so full of life that we all thought he was immortal.

Abid is the man of the family now and looks completely lost without Ali. Zainab is a widow. Ali's sons have lost a father. They will live with us, at least for now. We have laid out mats for them on the floor. Our children think it is like a party, having their cousins sleep in our house.

I have put aside half the money you sent for food. It will be enough to feed us for a few months at least. The other half, I am using to take a risk. You said I should spend it how I see fit, and I have taken you at your word.

Do you remember when I learned to spin and weave all those years ago? I have been going to the weaving group ever since, and I see now what I must do. I will start selling only khadi – a homemade cloth. I have had enough of paying more and more for British cloth, to sell to fewer and fewer British customers. We must focus on our own people. We must become self-sufficient.

I will teach Zainab too, and will source cloth from my

weaving circles. I've already begun building up a supply of khadi, and have found someone who makes fancier cloths as well. I have gotten others in the community to spread the word that when they need cloth, they must buy it from us. Zainab knows everyone, and people will listen to her. Of course, we will lose all of our British customers, and they will perhaps become angry that we are refusing to buy British materials. Naeem does not think this is a good idea, but it is my money (your money) that will see us through. Ali's death has shown me that enough is enough. We must save ourselves.

Except this time, you have saved us, Kathy. I hope you are not disappointed in how I am using your money. I hope you understand that I cannot stand by while our people starve and our brothers are sent to war. Our friendship is separate from my anger at your country's government. I hope you can understand.

Your friend,
Safia

Maryam re-read the page twice. *Ali has died in Libya* caught her each time – how basic and inadequate the sentence seemed to express something so awful. Evie looked at Maryam and ran her tongue round her braces. Wordlessly, she took the letter from her, folded it, and put it neatly at the bottom of the stack.

Maryam was nervous to read the last letter, afraid that Kathy was hurt and angry, and that their friendship would be fractured. Maryam thought Safia had done a very unwise thing: bitten the hand that fed her. She opened the final envelope.

23 August 1940

Dear Kathy,

Thank you for your kind words about Ali. I know he was sometimes hard on you, so it makes me happy to know that you remember him fondly. And I am sorry that things feel so difficult in Britain. I did not know that there was food and clothes rationing. There are rations here too. We cannot get enough rice or cotton, or even enough metal for the government to make money. When I go to Farooq uncle's shop, he often does not have coins and he gives me change in stamps. At least I have a use for them. I used five for this very letter. But even when we can get food, the prices are so high that we cannot afford much.

I am glad you understand why I do swadeshi. I believe in English you say boycott? We must have our own country and make our own decisions. I think you would feel the same if another country was using Britain in this way. If we go on like this, we will just get poorer and poorer, and we will never have the power to change anything. Do you understand?

Things here are becoming more frightening as well. The Indian National Congress and the Muslim League are fighting more and more, and violence continues to break out between Hindus and Muslims. Naeem gets nervous when I speak too much about swadeshi, because he says it is a 'Hindu matter'. I must remind him that we are one people. I sometimes wonder how we will build a new country together.

You must be very nervous for Gordon in France. I hope you have good news soon. And congratulations on your crossword competition. What was the mysterious letter you received from the government after winning? Perhaps you have met the Prime Minister? I must know!

Your friend,
Safia

So Kathy hadn't been angry. Part of Maryam relaxed despite the scary details in Safia's note.

'How strange,' Evie said. 'Why would anyone care about a crossword competition?'

Maryam shrugged. She was more interested in how the government could ever run out of metal to make coins. But none of these details offered any explanation of their coded letters.

'That's the last letter,' she said moodily. 'How will we ever figure out the code if there's nothing else? It just . . . ends.'

'We will,' Evie said with confidence. Maryam wasn't sure why Evie had such faith, but hoped she was right.

19. The Way Home

Maryam followed Evie down the aisle of the train and into two seats next to each other. Evie's mum, dad and brother took a table directly in front, and Zac sat up on his knees and turned around, peering over the chair at Maryam. His mum scolded him to face front and sit on his bottom, but Maryam saw him cast a curious glance back through the crack in the seats.

Evie had explained everything they'd learned in the letters to her mum and grandma over lunch, her dad and Zac struggling to keep up and jumping in with questions that she batted away impatiently. By the time they got to the end, everyone seemed awestruck, but couldn't explain how their coded letters fit in.

Maryam looked beyond Evie, sitting in the window

seat, out to the twilight sky, the last rays of sun streaking the horizon purple, the rest of the sky already dark although it wasn't even five. In the darkened window, she could see her ghostly reflection next to Evie's.

It made her think of their great-grandmothers. They were trying to understand them with only echoes and fragments.

Frustrated, she took stock of what they knew – loads about Safia and Kathy, and their lives at the beginning of the Second World War, but still nothing about what the letters in their folders meant. The letters had stopped suddenly, with Kathy getting a strange letter from the government after winning a crossword competition. Why had they switched to code? What did they have to hide?

Maryam pulled out a bag of sweets and offered one to Evie, who was checking her phone and jumped when Maryam waved the bag over her tray table. She took a red one and returned to her screen. Maryam thought she should probably leave her to it, but couldn't stop herself from speaking.

'So, we know so much about Safia and Kathy, but we still aren't any closer to knowing what the letters in the folders say.'

Evie put her phone face down on the tray table. 'Well, we are a *bit* closer,' she said. 'Like, we know that they were still friends when the war started, and that Safia's brother and Kathy's husband were both in the army. That seems like it could be something, right?'

Maryam considered it, and shook her head. 'I just get the feeling it was about *them*,' she said. 'Safia and Kathy – not the brothers or husbands. Besides, Ali died after less than a year in the army.'

Evie looked back out the window. Maryam hoped she wouldn't look at her phone again – she wanted to keep talking. But Evie just stared out at the night, her brow scrunched up.

Eventually, she turned back to Maryam and said, 'So, I was just thinking about this book I read last year. A murder mystery.'

'Uh huh,' Maryam said uncertainly.

'It got me thinking. In that book, the murderer left these notes full of numbers, where every number matched with a letter. What if these letters,' she gestured to the words in her folder, 'match up with other letters?'

Evie reached into her bag, got out paper and a pencil,

and proceeded to write the alphabet. 'Like, we know "Uvri" probably means "Dear".' She wrote U, V, R and I under D, E, A and R.

'We also know that your letters are from Kathy, and that's "Brkyp", and mine are from Safia, and that's "Jrwzr".' She filled these in and now had eleven letters. 'Maybe we can start with those and start making guesses at the words.'

A	R	N	
B		O	
C		P	
D	U	Q	
E	V	R	I
F		S	J
G		T	K
H	Y	U	
I	Z	V	
J		W	F
K	B	X	
L		Y	P
M		Z	

But Maryam's mind was doing the maths, and she

took the pencil from Evie and wrote a number above every letter of the alphabet, starting with A as 1.

1	2	3	4	5	6	7	8	9	10	11	12	13
A	B	C	D	E	F	G	H	I	J	K	L	M

14	15	16	17	18	19	20	21	22	23	24	25	26
N	O	P	Q	R	S	T	U	V	W	X	Y	Z

She went back to 'Uvri' and 'Dear'. D was 4 and U was 21. E was 5 and V was 22. Her heart sped up as she realised how simple it was. The code added seventeen to each letter to make a new letter. She stopped Evie, who had begun filling in the eleven letters she'd worked out.

'Look,' she said, showing her the number for each letter. 'We can get the whole alphabet – just add seventeen.'

Evie clasped Maryam's shoulder with a big grin. 'You're a genius!'

Maryam suppressed a smile. 'I'm really not,' she said. But her face warmed with pride.

Evie turned to the red folder, pulled the first sheet out, and started deciphering the letter on a new sheet of paper. Maryam opened her folder and did the same, marvelling at how first words and then sentences came up before her.

'I can't believe you figured it out,' Evie said, turning to Maryam.

'We both did,' Maryam said. 'I just can't believe we didn't see it sooner.' The code was remarkably simple – Hassan would be so annoyed that he hadn't seen it. But of course, this wouldn't be the first thing they talked about, Maryam realised with a return of the familiar tightening in her chest. How could it be, when their family was in crisis? Suddenly, she didn't want to go back home. She wanted to stay in the warm lighting of this train, working through the letters and learning their mysteries.

20. *Breaking the Bubble*

Evie had probably done the journey from Cambridge to London fifty times in her life, so knew without checking that they only had about thirty-five minutes left. She wrote out a cipher for herself, translating each letter to one seventeen spaces ahead of it. She worked as quickly as she could, but it went painfully slowly.

She'd resolved not to look at her phone again, and when it buzzed, breaking the bubble of her thoughts, she tried to ignore it. But then it buzzed again, and Evie gave in and picked it up.

Bella: Hey, do you have Mogyam's phone number?

Bella: As ur partners for the school project?

Evie shielded the phone and glanced over at Maryam,

who was staring blankly ahead, chewing on a sweet. She offered the bag, and Evie chose a red one and felt the gummy strawberry candy soften in her mouth. Evie turned her back to the window so the phone was out of view and quickly typed.

Evie: No, she doesn't have a phone.

She put the phone face down again, hoping that was it for now. She wanted to chuck her phone out the window, but also found it impossible to ignore for even a few minutes. It buzzed again and Maryam looked over with thinly disguised irritation.

Bella: Of *course* she doesn't 😁. Well can you get her address? I want to send her a little care package.

Evie: I'm at my gran's. Need to put my phone away.

Bella: OK, well when you get back then.

Whatever Bella was thinking, Evie knew she wasn't going to let it go. It would be easiest to just turn the address over, and maybe warn Maryam. Evie put the phone back in her bag and told herself she wouldn't look at it again for the rest of the journey. Maryam looked upset, staring at the back of the seat in front of her, seemingly in a trance.

'You OK?' Evie asked. She wondered if she had seen the messages.

'Yeah,' Maryam said, but Evie didn't quite believe her.

Evie turned back to the letter, but found it hard to focus. What if Maryam had seen not just that message, but all the other mean ones? She wished she'd just kept the phone in her bag.

Her mind wandered to Kathy and everything she'd learned about her. Kathy had already been through so much by her own age: her father was dead, she had moved to a new country, she felt like she didn't fit in. In a way, she was sort of like Maryam – a bit out of place.

Soon the train entered the tunnel into Kings Cross and as the scene outside the windows turned pitch black, Evie realised she'd barely managed to decipher any of the page in front of her. She looked over at Maryam, who was further ahead than she was, but had a much longer letter. As the train slowed to a stop, the passengers around them hurried to get up and Evie's parents signalled to them to start making their way off the train. Evie nodded, deciphering the rest of a sentence before putting the folder back in her backpack. Maryam waited in her seat, and the train was nearly empty by the time they made their way off.

Evie could see her parents looking back at them from the far end of the platform, impatient to get home, but Maryam dragged her feet. The cloud that seemed to have descended on her at the start of the train ride still hung over her.

'What's up?' Evie asked, wanting to seem empathetic, but mostly just feeling annoyed that she was moving so slowly.

Maryam looked back at the train, then up at the ceiling, as if looking for an escape hatch. 'It's just . . .' She paused. 'It's that I don't really want to go back home. Because . . .' Now she gestured with one hand, as if hoping to conjure the end of the sentence out of the air, and Evie began to feel nervous about what was coming. She waited for Maryam to confront her about the texts. 'Because things have been pretty rubbish lately. My parents are probably going to lose their shop.'

'Oh my God,' Evie said. She didn't know what else to

say. She felt self-absorbed for assuming the problem was her. 'Why?'

'The landlord is raising their rent. A lot.'

'Is that even allowed?' Evie asked. She turned to her parents and held up a finger to say they needed a minute.

'Yeah, it seems like it is,' Maryam said, seeming resigned. 'I'm not sure what they're going to do. They only have a month.'

Evie had seen Maryam look upset before, but not like this. It was like the fight had gone out of her. She picked at her cuticles, avoiding eye contact. Evie tried to think of a solution. What would her own parents do in that situation? In reality, they'd probably ask her grandparents if they could borrow the money, but that didn't seem like an option for Maryam.

'Have they talked to the landlord? Maybe they could ask for more time?' Evie suggested.

'Yeah, they tried that. He won't budge. It seems pretty hopeless, to be honest.' Maryam tugged on the straps of her backpack, as if to end the conversation. Evie turned to walk down the platform and Maryam hesitated behind her.

'I just don't know what's going to happen,' Maryam said softly. 'Anyways, that's why I might have seemed a little bit down on the train.' They fed their tickets into the machine and walked through the barrier into the large station foyer, where a group of carollers sang in front of a large tree. Zac and Evie's parents waited at the entrance to the tube, her dad pantomiming dragging them in with a big rope.

'I'm sorry,' Evie said. It felt like a totally insufficient response. 'Maybe we should tell my parents. They might have an idea.'

'No, please don't,' Maryam pleaded hastily. 'My parents would be so embarrassed if they knew I'd told you.' As they got close to Evie's parents, Maryam changed the subject abruptly. 'Hey, now that we know the code, let's work through these letters quickly – I'm scared we're going to lose them or something.'

'Yeah,' Evie agreed. 'Why don't you come over tomorrow and we can work on them?' she said. They descended the stairs and passed through the tube barriers, and from there, it was too loud and crowded to talk, so they sat in silence. Evie thought about what was happening to Maryam's family. There *must* be a solution. She still wondered if she should tell her parents – maybe they'd have an idea, or maybe they could help. But Maryam had been clear that she shouldn't.

When they climbed out of the station on the other side, there seemed to be nothing more to say, and when they parted ways in front of Maryam's gate, it was with an awkward hug. Evie decided she most definitely would not give Maryam's address to Bella. Then her phone buzzed.

Bella: Never mind – I've got a better idea anyway.

She didn't know what Bella was up to, but it wasn't anything good. She hoped, as she trailed behind her parents and Zac, that Bella wouldn't share her idea – she didn't want to know.

21. Decoding

When Maryam got home, she found Hassan hunched over his desk, a lamp with a too-bright bulb casting harsh light on his chemistry homework.

'How was it?' he asked.

'It was good,' she said uncertainly. 'It was . . . crazy, actually.'

She told him all about being caught out as Maryam, the letters they'd read, and about cracking the code.

Hassan shook his head as she spoke, a smirk spreading across his face until it was a disbelieving smile. 'So you and Evie are . . .'

'Actually connected, yes,' Maryam said, finishing his sentence.

'And her mum and grandma . . .'

'Know about the whole thing too. They were pretty amazed actually. Her mum kept looking at me like I was her long-lost daughter.'

Hassan laughed. 'At least you don't need to use your false identity any more.' He leaned back in his chair, tilting onto the back two legs. 'This is mad though. Maybe we can sell the story to Netflix.'

'Slow down, Hassan. We still have all these letters to decode.'

'I cannot believe the code was that basic,' he said, running his hands through his hair. 'I should have gotten it sooner.'

'Except you didn't,' Maryam said, laughing.

'So what are you waiting for, then?' Hassan asked. 'Let's do the rest of them.'

'Hassan, it takes *so long* to do each sentence.' She handed him the page she'd been working on. 'I've only done this much of the first one.'

Hassan scanned it and his eyes went wide. He opened his mouth to speak and Maryam talked over him in a panic.

'No, no, no! Don't tell me anything about what it says. I want to decipher the whole thing before I read it.'

She grabbed it back from him and he let it go, but said, 'OK, well can you do it now? Because what I just read is pretty . . . interesting.'

Maryam sat down with the page and the letter and worked through it, stubbornly refusing to look back at what she'd written until she was done. Hassan turned his attention to his homework, or pretended to.

After a while, Maryam announced 'Done!' and took the letter over to Hassan's desk. She slapped it down in front of him and they read it together.

Dear Safia,

I hope you are well, and that you've been able to decipher this letter. I feel like I've lived a lifetime in the past fortnight. I don't know where to begin! It all started with winning a crossword competition, and now here I am two weeks later, a codebreaker at Bletchley Park.

It looks silly when I write it — me, a codebreaker. And really, I shouldn't write it at all — what if someone read this letter?

I'll explain. Bletchley Park, or BP as everyone here

calls it, is a stately home in a small town where they've brought people — some mathematicians, and some ordinary people like me who are good at puzzles — to break the codes the Germans use to communicate with each other, and to attack the Allied forces. It's entirely secret, because of course we would be bombed if anyone knew what we were doing here.

Just before the break of dawn, new codes come through on machines that intercept them and help decipher them. The machines give us a starting point, but we have to do the rest. It's exciting — I feel, in a way, like I've been training for this my entire life. Sometimes I can crack them quickly, sometimes they take days. But so far I've cracked everything I've been given eventually. Some of the others have started calling me 'Egghead' — because I always crack. I'm still deciding whether I like it.

The others are nice, and fantastically clever. Many of them are mathematicians from Oxford or Cambridge, but I suppose they ran out of those and started finding people like me, or even students at school who are clever at maths. There are more women here than I would have thought, and some of them are still teenagers.

But it's all quite dangerous. I'm not allowed to tell anyone about the work, where we are, or even that it exists, lest the Germans catch wind of it and bomb us. I can't even tell Gordon. I am to tell anyone who asks that I am doing clerical work for the Royal Navy. It's an easy enough secret to keep, considering I don't see much of anyone outside of this place, except Rosemary and John, the elderly couple they've housed me with. But I needed to tell someone, and I felt like you'd appreciate what an unbelievable adventure I'm having.

Just before I left for BP, I received your last letter, opened and then taped shut. It was surely intercepted and checked by the government. They've done such an obvious job of opening it, it's as if they want me to know they're reading my post. So, we must communicate in code for now.

You would be fascinated by this place — the machines that take up entire rooms and do computations, the methods for working out the codes, the news we sometimes get that our work helped sink a German

U-boat. There are hundreds and hundreds of us here —
it's like a city.

I do hope you enjoy my decoy. I thought that if I
wrapped the letter in a recipe, whoever was checking
would just think it's women's stuff and wouldn't read
too closely beyond the first page. I don't expect you'll be
making a chicken pie anytime soon! But if you've gotten
this far, you've clearly understood the clue I wrote on the
recipe. Do write back, also using 17. I will then use 19
next time.

Kathy

Maryam came to the end of the page and looked up at Hassan, who was watching her expectantly.

'She was at *Bletchley Park?*' he finally said, agape.

'Yeah,' Maryam replied blankly. 'Wait, you've heard of Bletchley Park?' she asked, confused.

Hassan looked at her, frowning. 'You seriously *haven't*?'

Maryam raised her eyebrows and shook her head, as if to say *well, obviously not*. 'I mean, I can tell what it is from the letter, and Evie's grandmother mentioned it today, but . . . no, I haven't.'

'Well, it's famous,' Hassan said. 'Really famous. People say that the war might have lasted a couple of years longer if not for the codes they broke. And they, like, invented the first programmable computer.' He took out his history textbook, looked in the index for Bletchley Park, and handed the book over to Maryam, who read eagerly.

Maryam had suspected, but not quite *actually* believed there was a big, bombshell secret behind the letters.

'This is so mad!' Hassan said once she was finished. 'We're like two degrees away from someone important.'

'Hey, maybe Safia was someone important too!' Maryam said, feeling defensive of the woman she felt like she'd gotten to know.

'OK, sure,' Hassan conceded. 'I mean, we're all important, right? But your girl Kathy was like *history book* important.'

Maryam couldn't argue. But although it was Evie's great-grandmother who was part of something famous, it was she – Maryam – who had finally cracked the code. She was tempted to stay up and work through the rest of the letters herself, but it didn't feel right to do it without

Evie. Besides, she felt her eyelids drooping. She took her pyjamas into the bathroom, got changed, and sleepily brushed her teeth. When her head hit the pillow, she had no trouble falling asleep despite the harsh light of Hassan's desk lamp.

The next day after lunch, Maryam stood over Hassan's desk, arms folded around her red folder, her face both frustrated and pleading.

'Please just walk me there?' She had agreed with Evie as they got off the train that they would meet the following day – Sunday – at two p.m. to decode the letters. Now she needed Hassan to take her, because despite her persuasive arguments to her parents, she wasn't allowed to walk anywhere alone.

'I do have a *long* geography report to do, you know,' he said, but then added, 'but this is too mad to ignore. Plus I need to take my mind off things.'

She knew what he meant by 'things' and felt guilty again that she'd forgotten to worry about the shop that morning. But, once Hassan mentioned it, the pressure in her chest returned. The clock was ticking. What would they do when they ran out of time? What other jobs could her parents possibly get?

She heard a note of panic in her own voice as she said, 'Great,' with a smile, getting up and out of the room without missing a beat. She tossed Hassan's coat to him and put on her own puffy navy blue one, which used to be his. 'Mum, Hassan and I are going out,' she said.

'Where to?' her mum asked, poking her head out of the kitchen.

'Library,' Hassan answered before Maryam could. As they crossed the courtyard and headed through the gate, he said, 'I don't like lying but I didn't want to get into the whole thing now.' Maryam nodded. Even though there wasn't a reason to hide this from Mum, she didn't want to stop and explain from the beginning. And how could she explain that she needed to know how things had worked out for her great-grandmother because it gave her comfort that things might work out for them too?

They walked uphill to Howard Road, which sat at the top of the neighbourhood, in silence, their breath growing ragged. When they arrived at Evie's address, Hassan lingered back on the pavement.

'Come to the door with me,' Maryam said. 'Otherwise they'll think you're dodgy.'

Hassan looked at the Victorian stained glass front door. 'They'll think I'm dodge anyway. Look, they've got one of those video doorbells. I'll bet they're watching us right now.'

'Just come,' Maryam said, rolling her eyes. 'They're actually *nice*.' She saw the little camera turn towards them slightly as she stepped onto the doorstep and rang the bell. She had to admit it made her feel weird. She clutched the red folder between her fingers.

Evie's dad answered the door, wearing a brown jumper, jeans and clear plastic glasses on his head. 'Hello, Maryam. Do come in,' he said warmly. He then looked at Hassan with brief puzzlement before smiling and reaching out his hand. 'I'm Mark, Evie's dad.'

'Hassan,' Hassan mumbled, shaking his hand awkwardly. 'Maryam's brother.' He began to back away. 'Um, OK, I'll be going. Be back at five?'

Maryam nodded and stepped inside, but just as the door was closing behind her, Evie called down the stairs, 'Hassan, wait!'

Hassan, already at the gate, turned around reluctantly. Evie's dad looked at her with a frown as she skipped down the stairs.

'We need your help,' she said to Hassan. 'Zac is decoding but,' she dropped her voice to a whisper so Zac wouldn't hear, 'it's *slow*.'

'Uhh, I dunno ...' Hassan hesitated, looking at Maryam. 'I have a lot of homework to be getting on with.' Maryam shrugged back at him, not sure whether to urge him in or out.

'Right, of course,' Evie's dad broke in, 'GCSEs are serious business.'

Maryam could tell Evie's dad was less than keen on an older boy coming inside, but Evie ignored him.

'Dad, this is important work, and you and Mum have *meetings* and *can't help*.'

Her dad pursed his lips but didn't argue further. 'OK, well, you know the rules – door open.'

Maryam took in the hallway with black-and-white floor tiles and big framed pieces of art. As she peered back to the open-plan kitchen and lounge, and the big, leafy garden at the back, she reckoned that their entire flat could more than fit into Evie's ground floor. She imagined Hassan, who was looking around with an expression of extreme discomfort on his face, was thinking the same.

Maryam desperately hoped that Evie wouldn't mention anything to Hassan about the shop – she knew he'd hate that she'd told anyone.

In her room, Evie didn't say a word and took a seat at her desk, papers sprawled across the floor. Her little brother Zac sat with his back against her bed, his mop of sandy-coloured hair flopping in front of him as he slowly looked from the letter, to the cipher copied on a big sticky note, and then over to a lined page, where he copied the letter out in shaky, childish handwriting. He whispered each letter out to himself as he found it on the cipher.

'Hi,' Maryam said to him.

'Hi,' he said, without looking up, apparently not wanting to break his concentration. But, once he'd finished the word he was working on, he looked up at Maryam, his small blue eyes shining.

'I'm breaking the code!' he said proudly. 'I wanted to do it with my secret spy pen, but Evie wouldn't let me,' he added with disappointment.

'There's no point, Zac,' Evie said with annoyance. 'Then *we* wouldn't be able to read it unless we had the light on the end of your spy pen!'

Zac was suddenly distracted from the argument as his eyes went to Hassan. They went big for a moment and he looked straight back at the page he was working on. Maryam could see the tips of his ears go red.

'Yup, she brought a big boy with her,' Evie said to Zac. Then, turning to Hassan, she said in a stage whisper, 'He gets a bit shy around big boys.' Maryam felt embarrassed on Zac's behalf – older siblings could be so cruel sometimes.

'Hi.' Hassan waved down at him. 'I'm Hassan, Maryam's brother. What's your name?'

The paper seemed to be physically pulling Zac's head down to it, and when he looked up his face was crimson. 'Zac,' he mumbled.

'OK, Zac,' Hassan said, taking a seat next to him on the carpet. 'Since you know how to break this code, you're gonna have to show me.'

Maryam thought how brilliant Hassan had always been with little kids. Maybe it came from having a younger sister. Before she knew it, Zac was talking a mile a minute.

Maryam went over to Evie's desk, chomping at the bit to tell her what her letter had said. Evie bent over her red folder. 'It's more complicated than I thought,' she said. 'The cipher for each of the letters is different. It seems like each one moves the top row along two ticks.'

'I know,' Maryam started, 'because—'

But Evie didn't seem to hear her. 'For the first ones, we could just check it by making sure it started with 'Dear', so it was easy once you found what letter D lined up with. But after the first letters, they stopped using that, and their names too – they must have realised that that would be a shortcut to breaking the cipher. So you just need to see if it's making sense as you work it out.' She looked at Zac on her bed. 'I wrote out the cipher for the second letter back from Safia for him, and I'm working on the third.'

'Wow,' Maryam said, stunned with how Evie had worked everything out. 'Good job.'

Evie's eyes went to the folder in Maryam's hands. 'So, for the second letter from Kathy in your folder, you'll need to move the cipher two ticks on, and four ticks for the third. Can you explain that to Hassan?' She handed Maryam a stack of sticky notes and a sheet of lined paper. Maryam nodded.

'I don't need to. He already knows,' Maryam said.

'Wait, what?' Evie finally stopped, looked up, and turned around in her chair.

'I decoded the rest of the first letter last night and Kathy said that the first was seventeen and the next would be nineteen,' Maryam said, impatient to get to the bit she wanted to share. 'But that's not the news. The news is that Kathy was at Bletchley Park.'

She took out the deciphered letter and put it in Evie's hands.

'*What*?' Evie said, not yet looking at the letter, but rather at Maryam, to see if she'd heard right. Maryam nodded at the letter, urging Evie to read it.

She did, and when she'd finished, she said, 'My family are going to lose their minds.' She went on, 'Seriously. My dad is like *obsessed* with Bletchley. We've been there *twice*.' She looked back at the letter, disbelieving.

Maryam felt grateful that she'd deciphered the letter last night with Hassan, rather than having to ask Evie to explain what Bletchley Park was.

'Well, should we tell your parents?' Maryam asked.

Evie shook her head. 'Not yet. Mum is *dying* to know what's in them, but I want to finish them all first.' Maryam agreed – it would be better once they knew the whole story.

Maryam grabbed a stack of sticky notes and plopped down in a teal velvet beanbag chair in the corner. She shifted her weight around, the beans making loud rustling with each movement.

She first did as Zac and Evie had done and wrote out the cipher on a sticky note and stuck it at the top of the page. Then she got to work decoding, her eyes going from the letter, to the sticky note, to the paper and then back again. At first it was slow going, but by the end of the letter she'd sped up. But the next letter started with a new cipher and Maryam had to get used to it again. The letters got longer as she went – their great-grandmothers must have gotten more comfortable using the code. Hassan was the fastest of them all, and had finished the letters in Zac's pile while Evie worked through the final one in hers.

It took them nearly two hours to get through all the letters – five in each folder. When she finished, Maryam took her glasses off and rubbed her eyes. They put the originals back in their own folders and ordered the translations chronologically, just as they'd done with the letters in Cambridge, so they could see how the letters answered each other.

Evie's mum popped her head around the doorframe with a stealthiness that was either intentionally or unintentionally startling. Hassan jolted.

'Just checking if anyone needs a snack?' she asked.

Maryam was just about to say 'yes please' when Evie sighed dramatically and replied, 'Your spying is *obvious*, Mum. We're *fine*.' Evie's mum rolled her eyes and retreated back downstairs. Maryam wondered what the snack options were, but hid her disappointment.

Then, they read: Evie sitting at the desk and Maryam standing over her shoulder, who passed the page back to Hassan, who passed it to Zac, who pretended to understand but soon grew bored and wandered off. As Maryam worked her way through the letter in front of her, she glanced at Hassan from time to time, who looked back at her, stunned.

Safia, their own great-grandmother, had been part of

the movement for Indian independence. Maryam thought of Nani, who she'd never seen read a newspaper, let alone follow politics. But Nani's own mother had organised other women to make and sell their own cloth. It must have seemed like a hopeless battle – and she'd managed to make a living for her family while doing it. It just didn't sound like Maryam's family at all.

22. The Last Two Letters

Evie tried to get her head around what Kathy's letters told her. Kathy was a codebreaker. From the sound of it, she was gifted with numbers and patterns. She worked at Bletchley Park for three years, until the war ended. Then, she went back to Suffolk, Gordon came home, and she had a baby girl called Susannah. Gran.

She never told a soul about Bletchley Park – except Safia. By all accounts, she lived a normal, boring life. Evie found herself wishing that Kathy had carried on with secret missions after having Gran. And who was to say she didn't?

Eventually, Evie came to the last letter in her folder. It was written in English rather than in code, in scrawled, barely legible handwriting that was still clearly Safia's. It had been written on the back of some sort of advertisement, clearly in a hurry. It was dated 19 July 1947.

Dear Kathy,

I write in a rush as we leave for our train soon. In three weeks, India will have its independence. I cannot believe it. But it will come with the partition of India into two dominions: India and Pakistan. We need to choose. Pakistan is being created as an Islamic republic – a home for the Muslims of India. It is the place that is meant for us. And yet, it isn't my home. There is nothing for me there but a cousin I've never met. I am not sure we should leave, but Naeem is convinced it will be worse if we stay. We will need to leave our business, our home, everything. Millions of our people are crossing the country, not knowing where they are going. It is all so sudden.

Is this what I wanted? Is this better for my children? I cannot say. We will travel to Lahore and then to Karachi, where we will meet my cousin, who says there is a room for us to stay in. Perhaps we will return here one day. I have left our cloth, our furniture, and some of our things with Mrs Romesh next door for when we are able to come get them. Shehenaz is frightened. I am frightened too. I hope things

are better for her generation. I hope she can live without fear
and have everything she needs.

I will write to you from my new address once we have
arrived. Please do not write to this address, as we are leaving
now, before it is official and everyone begins to flee.

I hope Susannah is well and that you are enjoying
motherhood. And I hope you are finding a way to use your
very special brain. I will write to you soon.

Your friend,

Safia

Evie handed the letter across to swap with Maryam, who'd finished deciphering the last coded letter from Kathy in her folder. But Maryam just looked at Hassan, blinking. She handed her letter straight to him.

'What is it?' Evie asked eagerly, looking from Maryam to Hassan and back again. There seemed to be something Maryam was hesitant to show her, but she couldn't imagine what.

Hassan ran his eyes down to the bottom of the letter. When he'd finished, he puffed air out through his cheeks and handed it over to Evie. She grabbed it and read.

Dear Safia,

I hear that independence is coming for India. I know it has been the work of Gandhi and many others, but I can't help but think that it was regular people, people like _you_ who did it. You and your bravery in leading the women of Delhi and building your own business at great risk. You've always been a force to be reckoned with. Congratulations, Safia.

I wonder when the official transfer will happen? I am told it must be in the next year. The world is changing fast — new countries seem to be coming into existence every day. I hope the change coming in India brings everything you've hoped for. But what I've seen in the news makes me nervous too. Is it true that violence between Hindus and Muslims is growing? And that India might be divided up into two countries, one for Hindus and one for Muslims? What would that mean for you if it happened?

In news from my little life, motherhood is harder than I'd expected! I'm not sure how you've done this three times — I can barely manage once. Susannah is a wilful, hilarious little girl, and a constant hazard to herself.

I suppose part of me is melancholy to leave codebreaking behind. I liked making my own salary and doing something meaningful. Now I sometimes feel like my life is all about serving Susie and Gordon. Of course, raising a child is important, but who knows if I'm any good at it. I hope it will be different for this baby when she grows up — I hope she'll be able to do what she wants without there being a war on.

But look at me, being self-indulgent again. I do know I have plenty to be grateful for. I feel ever so spoilt writing to you and moaning, whilst your problems are of a different scale entirely. Please continue to tolerate me!

I must admit that I worry about you. I think often about how, despite the war and everything that came with it, I believe my child will be safe in this country. I want yours to be safe too. I'm going to send you something that I want you to think of as an insurance policy — use it now if you need to, or keep it for the future. It's a sapphire I inherited from my father. I got plenty of baubles from him, but I know this sapphire came from India. I like the idea of sending it home. I'll post it in a separate package. Please do let me know that it's gotten to you.

Yours truly,

Kathy

Evie furrowed her brow and looked at Maryam. 'So does your grandmother have this bauble? Have you ever seen it?'

'No, I don't think Nani has any sapphires,' Maryam said. All of Nani's jewellery was twenty-four carat gold, in an ornate style that clearly hadn't come from Britain.

'Look at the date on the letter,' Hassan urged. 'Kathy's was sent just two days before Safia's. Maybe she didn't get the news that Safia had moved until after she'd sent the sapphire.' Evie looked – he was right. Kathy's was dated 17 July 1947.

With a sinking feeling, she realised what that meant. Kathy wouldn't have received the letter. 'So by the time the sapphire got there, Safia already would have been gone.'

Hassan nodded.

'And then what would have happened to it?' she asked.

He shrugged. 'Likely someone else nicked it.'

Evie had never known this sapphire had existed, so she knew it was silly to feel like its loss was a tragedy. But a phrase Gran often said popped into her head and she said it out loud. 'What a waste.'

23. A Lost Jewel

Maryam's mind raced. Kathy had wanted to give the jewel to Safia, to be passed down to Nani and kept in the family. She'd called it 'an insurance policy'. And now that her family needed it, it was probably lost for ever.

But was it? What if they could find it somehow? And if they did, would Evie's family agree that it was rightfully theirs?

Hassan's face was apprehensive. It was a face that said *this could get awkward.*

But Evie didn't look anxious at all – just stunned. 'We've got to find that jewel,' she said. 'It belongs to you.'

'Hassan is right,' Maryam said quickly. 'Someone probably stole it. A neighbour, the postman. People were desperate.'

But Evie didn't seem to be listening. She got up from her chair and paced around her room. Then, she took her phone out and began to photograph each page they'd decoded.

'What are you doing?' Maryam asked. The decisiveness of Evie's actions made her feel hopeful, like there was a plan.

'I'm going to send these to my gran. Maybe she knows what jewel it is. If it's a family heirloom, she might be able to tell us more about it.'

Maryam felt the hope drain out of her as she realised that, even if Evie's grandmother knew which pendant Kathy had been referring to, she was unlikely to have it. And even if it was somewhere in her house, she was unlikely to agree that she should give it to Maryam's own family. Evie's grandmother had been helpful in Cambridge, but Maryam didn't get the impression that she was likely to part with a family heirloom.

'Evie, wait. You don't have to – it was a million years ago,' she said, glancing at Hassan, who nodded reluctantly. But Evie ploughed on.

'Don't be ridiculous. That letter is clear as to what Kathy

wanted. And besides, you guys *need* it,' she said. Maryam avoided Hassan's stare, but could see his eyebrows raised, more surprised than angry to see that Maryam had told Evie about their trouble with the shop. 'I'm going to need to explain the whole thing to Gran – Bletchley Park, the pendant, all of it.' Evie was still snapping on her phone, while gesturing towards the letters. 'I don't think she knows any of . . . this.'

Once she was done, Evie began ordering the deciphered letters so Maryam could take them to Nani, and then stopped. 'Oh, hey,' she said, 'there's one more in Kathy's folder. And it's in English.'

Maryam and Hassan came over to the desk and read the short letter, which was written in halting English on a small sheet of paper, in a different handwriting than Kathy's or Safia's.

4 June 1948

Dear Kathy,
   I write to tell you the sad news that Safia is dead. She had

tuberculosis and died quickly. I am sorry my English is not good so I do not write more. You were a good friend to Safia and she loved you. Thank you for all you did for our family and I wish you a good life.
   Kind regards,
   Naeem Sharif

Maryam knew this was how it ended. It shouldn't have felt surprising. And yet, the sadness of Safia's death hit her in the gut. She thought of Nani, a child in an unknown place, now without her mother. She thought of what Nani had told her – that they'd always intended to go back to Delhi, but they never did. For the first time, it hit Maryam how inconceivably sad that was. Her nose burned. She took a tissue, only partly used, from her pocket, and dabbed it.

'Are you OK?' Evie asked. Maryam nodded, sniffed and put the tissue in the wastepaper basket.

'Why does everyone seem so depressed?' Zac, who had drifted back into the room, asked. 'This is boring.'

'So go do something else, then,' Evie said irritably, and Zac headed downstairs, fidgeting with his slap band. Evie turned to Maryam. 'I'm sorry about Safia.'

It was weird, because she had never known Safia, who died long before her own mother was even born. But she also appreciated Evie saying it, because she did feel sad. Sad for whom? She wasn't sure. For Nani, she supposed, and for all of the pain that had been caused.

Maryam and Hassan stood up slowly, still trying to process everything they'd learned. 'I guess we should go,' Hassan said.

'My gran's not going to believe it,' Evie said, typing a text to her grandmother and sounding a thousand miles away. Then, brightening with an idea, she added, 'Hey, we should get our grandmothers to meet each other. Like, a Grandma Summit!'

Maryam smiled and nodded vaguely as she remembered the expression on Evie's mum's face when Nani had come to the door of their flat. She glanced at Hassan, who gave her a look that said *these people will think Nani is strange.*

Maryam responded as if he had said it out loud. 'But

their mums were friends for their whole lives. They've *got* to meet.' Maryam was done caring if anyone thought they were strange. If there was one thing she'd learned that week, it was that it truly didn't matter in the grand scheme of things.

They agreed that they'd each talk to their grandmothers that evening, show them the decoded letters, and make a plan for them to meet. Evie gave the full set of letters to Maryam to take home.

Maryam suddenly imagined Evie's parents reading the letters and Evie explaining to them that they needed to find the jewel because Maryam's family desperately needed the money. Evie would be trying to help, but she couldn't bear the thought of more people talking about her family with pity.

'Hey, could you maybe not show your parents the one about the jewel?' Maryam could tell from the frown on Evie's face that winning her parents over was part of her plan. 'At least, not yet?'

Evie hesitated, then said, 'OK.'

Downstairs, they thanked Evie's parents, and passed Zac playing a video game on their way out. Hassan tore off a piece of paper, wrote something down, and passed it to a confused Zac.

'Cheat code, my man,' he said, and left Zac beaming with gratitude.

Outside, it was fully dark and the air felt crisp. The Christmas lights on the houses on Evie's street twinkled and Maryam hugged herself, feeling satisfied – with having figured out what was in the folders, with the chilly breeze and twinkling lights, and with the little bubble of hope weighing against the big bubble of despair that had been with her the past couple of weeks.

'So we're gonna show these to Nani tonight?' she asked Hassan.

'That's what we said, innit?'

'Don't say "innit". That's not even how you talk,' Maryam huffed.

'Innit though,' Hassan said, winding her up. She couldn't help laughing.

'No, but seriously – what if she doesn't want to see them?' Maryam asked. 'Like, what if reading all of this is too upsetting for her?' This had been fun and interesting for them – a mystery to solve – but it had also made them sad. To Nani, it was one of the hardest parts of her life, dragged up and put under her nose.

Hassan considered this. 'Well, there's only one way to find out. Ask her. Just maybe hold back the one about the heirloom sapphire. Just in case.'

He had a point. Evie hadn't even told her family about the pendant yet.

'And what do you think about the jewel?' Maryam asked, now that they were alone.

Hassan made a dismissive face, halfway between a smirk and a frown. 'Look, Mari, I know Evie is your friend, but don't go getting your hopes up.' Maryam felt the little bubble inside her burst, replaced by annoyance at being talked down to, and embarrassment that she *had* gotten her hopes up. 'Even if they find the sapphire, people like them? They've got lawyers and pre-nups and whatnot. They don't play around with the family jewels – especially if it wasn't made official in Kathy's will.'

They walked downhill, through the gate to their block, and across the courtyard. Maryam hoped Hassan was wrong, but feared he was right.

24. The Final Project

As she approached the gates to St Mary's, Evie thumbed through the stack of Christmas cards she'd written to her friends, wondering if exchanging cards on the last day of term was a tradition she should have outgrown. She was relieved to see Zoe reach into her backpack and take out an envelope with her name on it, and with a chocolate taped to the front.

'Merry Christmas!' Zoe said with a smile.

'Thanks,' Evie said, feeling more excited than she should. She sorted through the pile and handed Zoe hers. 'Here you go.'

'Open yours!' Zoe said eagerly.

Evie ripped open the envelope and took out the card, which said *Meowy Christmas*, and had a grumpy looking cat on it. Zoe thought grumpy cats were hilarious, maybe because she had one herself. Evie peeled the foil off the chocolate and ate it instantly. Laughing, she said, 'Now you open yours.'

When Zoe saw that her card also said *Meowy Christmas*, with a slightly different grumpy cat on the front, she laughed so explosively she snorted.

When their giggling died down, Zoe said, 'So that's so weird that you weren't on the tube with anyone else on Saturday! My mum *swore* there was another girl there who you were talking to.'

Evie tried to keep a shade of a smile on her face. 'Huh. That *is* weird.'

'She said she looked Asian?'

They were entering the school gates and Evie desperately wished Zoe would let it go. 'Maybe it was someone muttering to herself but she *looked* like she was talking to me. You know, you get all sorts on the tube.'

Zoe shrugged and they parted ways at the foot of the stairs. Evie trudged up to Mr Whipple's classroom to find him hunched behind his computer, wearing a hat shaped like a Christmas pudding, which did not suit him. His slightly sad expression contrasted ridiculously with the custard-topped pudding perched on his head. She popped over to Bella's table, gestured towards Mr Whipple's hat and mouthed 'Wow,' handing Bella her card.

'Ooh!' Bella said, accepting it, then flipping through her stack to find Evie's. The envelope had Evie's name written on the front in perfect 3D block letters, and the space around her name was coloured in a bright red-and-green pattern.

'Oh, Bella, it's beautiful,' Evie said. She looked at the fat stack that sat on Bella's desk. 'It must have taken you ages to do all these.'

Bella eyed the envelopes in Evie's hands. 'Who are you giving those to?' she asked.

Evie looked down at the couple of cards in her hands, one to Ted and one to Maryam, and felt relieved that their names were written on the opposite side.

Ignoring the question, her eyes wandered across Bella's table to a large, spiral-bound scrapbook in front of her. Evie got a sinking feeling in her stomach. The scrapbook said *Our Family Learning Journey* on the front in colourful letters. Her gaze then darted around the rest of the room, where she now noticed that everyone else had big, rolled-up posters or dioramas on their desks.

'Oh no,' she groaned aloud. 'It's today, isn't it? Our project is due.'

Bella nodded and looked at her with sympathy. 'You forgot?' she asked, stating the obvious. Evie nodded.

'You should pretend you're sick and go home,' Bella suggested. It wasn't the worst idea.

Evie went to her table. How could she have forgotten that they needed to present their final family tree project today? She'd been so wrapped up in the letters that it had completely slipped her mind.

She slid into her seat and rolled her eyes at the papier-mâché tree that sat between Ted and Leo.

'Let me guess,' she said with scorn to Leo, 'your nanny was working overtime this weekend.'

He fist-bumped Ted, who looked slightly embarrassed. Evie tucked Ted's Christmas card into her bag – she'd give it to him later. The forgot-my-homework feeling spread through Evie's body. Her mind grasped for a way out. Could she call Mum and get her to fake a family emergency?

She was so wrapped up in her panic that it took her a

moment to notice what was in front of Maryam's empty seat: a pyramid of tins of cat food, adorned with a bow. Evie's stomach curdled with dread. In a heartbeat, she thought she should hide the tins away before Maryam arrived, but in the next heartbeat the door swung open and Maryam walked in. The rest of the class, who had spotted the tins before Evie, watched with anticipation as Maryam took her seat. She looked at the cat food, then at Evie, questioningly. Evie turned her palms up and shook her head, as if to say *I didn't know.*

'Look what the cat dragged in,' said Leo, snorting through his nose at his own joke. It got titters around the classroom.

Evie met Maryam's eyes. Maryam stared back steadily, as if testing her. As if searching for a sign that she might be in on the joke. Seeming not to find one, Maryam blinked and took a breath.

'I thought from the cat food that I was meant to be the cat. But am I actually supposed to be what the cat dragged in?' She looked at the cat food, rather than Leo, as she said this in a mock-perplexed voice. No one responded, and she put the six cans into her backpack and sat down.

Evie wasn't sure what to say. Maryam got out her pen and book as usual. Failing to get any sort of reaction, everyone else slowly turned back to their tables.

'I didn't know,' Evie said in a forceful whisper.

'I believe you,' Maryam replied in a flat tone that Evie couldn't read. Maryam had dealt with it so calmly that Evie wondered what she was feeling inside. She decided to change the subject.

'So, we totally forgot about the project.' Evie broke the news in a low voice, hoping that it wouldn't completely upend the sense of calm Maryam had managed to put on.

'Well, not *totally*. I remembered last night, but it was too late to make anything,' Maryam said, opening her book. 'So . . . I wrote us a scene to perform.' She passed a sheet of paper across the table as if she was handing Evie a surprise birthday gift. It had lines written out for each of them. Evie felt her mood go from panicked to relieved to panicked again as she thought about acting out a two-person scene with Maryam in front of the class. She realised she'd rather fail the assignment. This was exactly what she hadn't wanted.

'Uh, I don't know,' Evie said hesitantly. 'I don't think

anyone else is doing a . . . performance.' She struggled to find a way to tactfully say *now they're going to make fun of both of us.*

'So what?' Maryam asked. 'It will be original. The only other option is presenting on what we found in the folders, and I'd really rather not. It just doesn't feel right.'

Evie agreed. The folders were too special to share with the whole class – she wanted to keep them just for her, Maryam and their families. She scanned the scenes that Maryam had written. The first was of Safia and Kathy in Delhi, the second of Safia going to an independence rally, the third was of Kathy making wartime recipes. A couple of months ago, Evie would have feigned illness and left Maryam to do her scenes alone. But now, she couldn't quite bear to abandon her.

'Right.' Evie relented, breathing out through puffed cheeks and preparing herself for the banter she'd be sub- jected to at breaktime. Then, remembering her manners, she said, 'Anyhow, thanks for doing it.'

Eventually their turn came and Maryam hopped out of her seat. Evie edged around the desk and made her way to the front of the class as hesitantly as possible, trying to signal to the class that this wasn't her idea and she didn't really want any part in it. She dragged her feet to a spot a few feet away from Maryam.

'Our research took us back to colonial India, when the British ruled, and before Pakistan existed as a country, to Delhi, where our great-grandmothers both lived,' Maryam began in a formal-sounding stage voice that she projected across the classroom. Evie cringed.

Maryam had memorised her lines, which she delivered in her unnaturally loud and well-articulated voice. She kept looking at Evie and clearing her throat when it was her turn. Evie read her lines quickly from the page, which only seemed to make Maryam slow down.

When they were finished, hands went up for questions, the first from a boy at the back, named Alfie.

'Were there any scenes that you felt went . . . *astray*?' He smirked and the rest of the class cracked up. Evie and Maryam shook their heads grimly and Mr Whipple called on a boy named Nathan.

'I just wanted to say that I found that performance *hiss*-terical.' Evie stared at the ground, inching towards her seat, trying to physically remove herself from the space. At last, Mr Whipple told them they could go ahead and sit down.

Well, the worst the class could give them wasn't actually that bad, Evie thought, relieved that it was over.

'Not going to win any Baftas, is it?' Maryam muttered to herself. She looked slightly annoyed. Evie instantly regretted how embarrassed she'd felt, and that she hadn't tried harder to do the performance justice.

'Sorry that I was . . . a bit pants up there,' Evie said. 'I'm just not very good with performing.' This was a lie. She was usually fine with it – she didn't mind speaking in front of people – her only problem was with being associated with something she knew their classmates would find tragic. And yet, Maryam's work had saved her skin. She was relieved that Ted and Leo were getting up to go next, so they didn't have time to make any obnoxious remarks.

'That's OK,' Maryam said. 'At least we did *something*.' She seemed pretty unaware that they were the joke of the class. Maybe she was used to it by now, or maybe she just didn't care. Evie wondered to herself whether this was a good or bad thing. But Maryam was right – it had been better than faking an illness in the end.

While Ted and Leo were away from the table, Evie decided to say what was playing on her mind. 'I'm sorry about the cat food. That was mean.'

'Did you really not know about it?' Maryam whispered back.

Evie shook her head. Maryam seemed only to care whether Evie had betrayed her.

'I'm not even sure I get it?' Maryam said. 'What's the cat food for? I'm . . . like a cat?'

Oh, Evie realised with a pang in her chest, *I'm going to have to explain what the joke is.* She wondered if it would be cruel or kind to do so. Either way, she felt like she should come clean.

'So, remember that time you hissed at Bella?' she asked, and instantly saw the penny drop as Maryam nodded slowly and hummed her understanding. 'Right, so that's the joke.' Evie wanted to stop there – it was enough for Maryam to understand – but knew she had to go further. 'And . . .'

She couldn't find the right words, but Ted and Leo were wrapping up their presentation, so she had to keep going.

'There's something I want to confess, and it was from

back before I really knew you.' The more she spoke, the more anxiety she saw creep into Maryam's face. She ran her tongue over her braces and pressed on. 'On the day you hissed at Bella, I . . . I made a dumb joke.' Maryam stared, unblinking, and bit her lip. 'I called you . . . Mogyam. And it sort of stuck – with Bella, anyway.'

Maryam looked away, and Evie couldn't tell if she was more hurt or angry. She hoped Maryam would forgive her, and searched her face for clues of whether she would. But Maryam's face was flat, so Evie kept talking to fill the silence.

'Look, I'm sorry. Really sorry. I wouldn't have done that if I'd known you. And I swear I wasn't part of the cat food thing.'

Maryam seemed to have made her decision and turned back to Evie. 'Well, I'm glad you told me. Thanks for that.'

Leo and Ted were making their way back to their seats. Evie took out the Christmas card. 'Here,' she said, handing it to Maryam, hoping to change the tone a bit. Maryam's face lit up as she accepted it, and then fell a bit as she opened it. Evie had forgotten what the card said: *Meowy Christmas.*

Evie drew in breath. 'I didn't . . .'

But Maryam saw her face and the corners of her mouth turned up again. Then she stifled a laugh that came out first through her nose and then in a little giggle. Evie felt it too, the sheer ridiculousness of it, as she looked at the grumpy cat on the card and thought about the tins of cat food in Maryam's bag, and her belly started to convulse with giggles. Mr Whipple spun around in his chair and looked at them, and Evie put her hand over her mouth, giggling all the more.

'Thanks,' Maryam said. 'I like it.'

As they packed their bags at the end of form, Evie said, 'So, my gran is coming over on Sunday. Can your grandmother still come?'

'Yup, she can,' Maryam said. Then, hesitantly, she asked, 'Did you speak to your grandmother about . . . you know . . . ?' She trailed off, but Evie knew what she was asking. The jewel. She was ashamed to say she hadn't, but it wasn't for a lack of trying.

'Not yet,' she said, and, seeing Maryam's expression freeze, quickly added, 'but I will. I texted Gran all those photos of the letters, but she said she couldn't possibly read them on a screen, so she was going to go to the Post Office and print them out. I'll talk to her tonight.' Seeing that Maryam looked uncertain throughout her long explanation, she added, 'Promise.'

But the truth was, Evie knew that Gran wouldn't be rushed into anything. She needed to leave her to read the letters and understand what was in them. She just hoped Gran would find the story as remarkable as she did.

25. Nani Reads the Letters

Maryam had asked Nani, then asked her again, whether she was sure she wanted to read the letters. She kept warning her that they were quite sad, until Nani grew exasperated and said, 'Mari, I want to read them!' So, she'd given Nani the homework of reading all of the letters between Safia and Kathy – both the early ones and the coded ones, fifteen in all – that day whilst she was at school.

Nani was a slow reader in English and Maryam doubted she'd have finished, but when she and Hassan walked through the front door and down the corridor, they found her sitting at the dining room table, the letters in a neat stack in front of her, waiting for them with a cup of tea that smelled of cardamom and a plate of cumin biscuits. When she saw them, she sat up straight and eagerly gestured to the spots at the table in front of her.

'Just a second,' Maryam laughed, putting her bag down and getting a glass of water. Hassan sat at the other end of the table with a chemistry book and a calculator.

'I'm gonna listen, but I've got to get on with this homework,' he said.

Nani patted his hand in approval and offered Maryam a biscuit.

'So,' Maryam said, taking one, 'did you finish?' The minute she took a bite she remembered, again, that she didn't like little cumin seeds in her biscuits.

'Of course I finished,' Nani said indignantly. 'How could I not? My own amma's thoughts, right there before me. It was like I could hear her voice in those letters.'

Maryam thought, for a moment, what it would be like if her own mum died. She thought she'd probably want to banish the memory from her mind, never to revisit it. But then again, maybe reading the letters would be like getting to speak to her mother again. Maryam quickly shook away the thought, forcing it out and replacing it with an image of Mum as she had seen her this morning, healthy and energetic.

'Was any of it surprising?' she asked Nani. 'Like, is how life sounded in the letters how you remember it?'

Nani took a sip of tea and considered this. 'Yes and no,' she said at last. 'I remember the Delhi she was writing about. I remember our flat and my parents' market stall. I also knew there was an English woman who sent Amma letters, but I didn't know she sent money. And I didn't know my parents were so afraid. When you are a child, your parents hide their fears from you, but I saw them here,' she said, patting the letters. 'She was so afraid for what would happen to us.'

Hassan stopped pretending to work and looked up. 'Did you know that she was, like, a revolutionary?'

Nani waved him away with her hand. 'Pshhh. Revolutionary? I wouldn't say that. But no – I learned about Ghandi and the *swadeshi* movement in school. It was in our history books, although maybe not in yours. I did not know that my amma had anything to do with it,' Nani said.

'OK, not a revolutionary. Just, you know, *supporting the revolution*.' Hassan smiled to himself and then went back to acting like he was working out a formula.

'But Nani, didn't your dad ever tell you about any of it, like what they did with their business or the money Kathy sent?' Maryam asked.

Nani took a slow bite of her biscuit, wiped a crumb from her mouth and took another sip of tea. 'He didn't like speaking about her after she died. He didn't like speaking about our old life in Delhi, either. Needing to leave and then my amma dying were very hard on my abbu. It was hard on all of us, but him especially.'

Maryam reached across the table, put her hand on Nani's and squeezed it. Maryam realised that there was so much she didn't know. So much existed in Nani's head that she hadn't shared, and if no one ever asked, it would just disappear. Maryam was suddenly conscious that she wanted to get as much information out of Nani as possible.

'So, what happened next?' she asked. 'You know, after the last letter. After your mum ...' She trailed off, not wanting to say 'died'.

'We stayed in Karachi. Abbu was never really able to get his business going again after we moved. He didn't know anyone, and had trouble getting customers or finding ways to source cloth. But Faisal, my eldest brother, had trained as a mechanic and Saleem, my next brother, was working as a builder. So, they helped support us while Abbu did what he could.'

Maryam did the maths in her head. Nani's brothers would have been . . . maybe fourteen and sixteen? When Hassan did a week of work experience last year, Nani had gone on a rant about how children should be focusing on their education, not working. She and Hassan had laughed about it – he'd said 'off to the sweatshop for another day of child labour' before leaving to stack boxes at the sports shop – but Maryam understood now why it had touched a nerve for Nani. She didn't want her own grandchildren to have to work like her brothers did.

'If things were so hard in Karachi, why didn't you just go back to Delhi?' Maryam asked.

Nani made a noise that was almost like a laugh, but didn't have any joy in it. 'We couldn't. Pakistan was the country for Muslims. We felt safer there.' She seemed like she was going to say something else but just shook her head. 'My memory of Delhi soon faded, and it wouldn't have been the same without Amma anyhow. And when I was fifteen, I became engaged to marry Hafeez, your grandfather.'

'Fifteen?' Hassan choked, nearly spitting out his biscuit.

'Yes,' Nani said with a chuckle. 'Things are different back home, and they were even more different then. We had a happy marriage. Maybe you will too just next year!'

Hassan dropped his pencil in disbelief and opened his mouth to protest, when Nani smiled and said gently, 'Come on, I'm joking.'

She folded her hands in front of her as if the story was finished, but Maryam and Hassan kept looking at her until she said, 'Well, you know the rest, don't you? Hafeez and I saved our money, and our whole community contributed, and we were able to buy two plane tickets to London. We stayed with friends of relatives, and worked in restaurants, and eventually we were able to open the shop with our friend Bashir. And then he passed on, and he didn't have any children, and so we kept running it.'

At the mention of the shop, the sick feeling in Maryam's stomach came back and burned up through her chest. After all those years, it could be gone. The thought of this made each of them lose their words. When Hassan spoke, he asked about something entirely different.

'Do you think your mum would have been sad that you moved here?' he asked. 'You know, after she wanted independence from Britain so much?'

Maryam bristled at the directness of the question, but also looked to Nani for her answer. Her mother had sacrificed her livelihood for independence from the British, only to have Nani move to Britain a few years later.

Nani was shuffling through the letters, looking for something. Suddenly, she found it, and held the page a bit away from her face so she could read it. 'Here,' she said, reading aloud from Safia's letter. 'She said, "I hope things are better for her generation. I hope she can live without fear and have everything she needs".' She put the letter back in the pile, having made her case. 'Her hopes for me came true, you see? I am safe and I have what I need.' She looked at each of them in turn. 'You do too. That would have made Amma happy.'

But did they? Maryam wondered whether they'd have what they needed for much longer. It had been money, pure and simple, that had got Safia and her family through the hard times. And it was money that they needed now.

The lock turned in the door and they knew from the way she hung up her coat and slipped off her shoes that it was Mum. She stopped at the entrance to the dining room and looked at the three of them.

'What's going on?'

Maryam looked at Hassan and then at Nani, who pushed the stack of papers in front of an empty chair. 'Sit. We have a good story to tell you.'

26. Grandma Summit

Evie's gran fussed around in their kitchen, looking for a teapot. She seemed a bit nervous, which wasn't like her.

'How could you not have a teapot?' Gran asked Mum.

'We definitely have one somewhere. We just don't use it that often. We usually just make tea in mugs,' Mum said defensively. Evie's gran scoffed and pulled over a stool, standing on it to reach to the back of the cupboard. She pulled out an old yellow teapot that Evie had never seen before.

'Here,' Gran said, putting it on the counter. 'Now where's your tea cosy?' Mum rolled her eyes and left the room.

Evie shrugged. 'I don't know what that is,' she answered helplessly. She went into the pantry and took out an unopened box of biscuits – the kind with chocolate on top. She opened the packet and laid out the biscuits in a circular pattern on a plate, hoping to distract herself from the nervousness in the air.

She had explained everything to Mum the previous night, and Mum had gone from awestruck to excited to anxious about guests coming over. She had held back the final letter like she'd promised Maryam, and she was glad there wasn't an additional thing to work Mum into a frenzy.

Meanwhile, Evie was growing impatient to speak to Gran. She'd sent her the photos of the letters, Gran had printed them out and Evie had sent her a message asking if she'd read them. All she'd written back was *Yes. We can speak properly when I am in London.*

When she'd read the message, Evie's pulse had sped up. She had been buzzing with anticipation of her gran's shock at the news, but instead her message showed no hint of wonder or excitement. She feared that Gran thought the whole thing was an elaborate hoax. Now here she was, in Evie's kitchen, half an hour before Maryam was due to arrive, and she still didn't seem in any rush to start the conversation.

Evie sat down at the table and waited, but Gran just kept counting out teaspoons and saucers.

'Gran?' she ventured. 'Do you think we could chat about the letters now?'

Gran didn't turn around, but replied irritably, 'Do just wait whilst I get things organised.'

Evie blew air out of her cheeks and sat with her hands folded. Slowly, Gran took a brown folder from the kitchen island and hobbled over to the table. She sat down and carefully removed the printed copies of the letters, putting them in a thin stack in front of her.

'Well?' Evie prodded. 'What did you think?'

Gran took a big breath. 'What do I think?' she said, as if asking herself. 'It's really something,' she said, running her hands over the pages. 'It's almost entirely new to me, and quite unbelievable.'

Evie wondered whether Gran meant 'unbelievable' like 'really amazing' or 'unbelievable' like 'I literally don't believe this is the truth'. She decided to wait for Gran to say more, which she eventually did.

'It is unbelievable that my mother was part of one of the most impressive things our country ever did. I couldn't be more proud,' she said, looking down and fiddling with a napkin. She took a breath and Evie could see that she was trying to stay composed. 'She kept the biggest event of her life a secret. You see, that's just what that generation did. Never bragged, never told a soul except Safia. I didn't know how important that friendship was to her. There was so much I didn't know.'

Gran looked out the back window, her foggy blue eyes sad. Evie hadn't considered how strange it would be for her to learn how much of her own mother's life had been a secret.

Evie snuck her hand onto the plate and took a biscuit. Gran looked at her with pursed lips, but didn't stop her.

'It's pretty wild that your mum and Maryam's grandmother's mum were friends, isn't it?' Evie asked, trying to move on to Maryam's family.

'Indeed, it is *wild*,' Gran said, saying the final word with mockery. 'As you get older, you'll learn how small the world is. Eat that over the sink, will you, or you'll get crumbs everywhere.'

Evie obliged, but grew frustrated as she chomped her biscuit. Surely Gran was going to show a *bit* of excitement?

She wondered if she was intentionally avoiding the topic of the jewel because she didn't have it, or because she didn't want to give it up.

After a minute, Gran went on.

'I'm sure you know she became a maths teacher? My mother, I mean.'

Evie nodded, perplexed at the transition. Gran rifled through the papers, pushed her glasses onto her head, and put on her reading glasses, which hung on a chain around her neck. Eventually she found what she was looking for.

'Here, this one,' she said. 'Something clicked when I read this line that Safia wrote in her last letter: *I hope you find a way to use that special brain of yours.*' Gran looked up, peering over her glasses at the end of her nose. 'See, I think that changed my mother. It wasn't until after that that she started training to teach. Back then, women didn't usually go back to work after they had children, let alone start a new career.'

'Wow,' Evie said. All she had grown up knowing about her great-grandmother was that she was a teacher. It was strange that she'd lived a whole life before that.

'So you see,' Gran went on, speaking with more animation now, 'I think Safia challenged her to go for it.'

Evie nodded. But Gran wasn't finished.

'It changed the rest of her life. And you know, I think having that friend through all those years brought her a lot of joy. I just wish I knew what happened to Safia after the letters ended, and I intend to ask her daughter today. When I give her this.'

Without warning, she took something out of the brown envelope and held it up. It was a sapphire pendant. She let it dangle from her hand.

Evie looked from Gran, who had a bit of mischief in her grin, to the glittering stone. It was bright blue, tear-drop shaped, and larger than anything she'd seen outside a museum. Around the sapphire were clusters of white diamonds. Evie felt a smile involuntarily spread across her face and came close to it, captivated.

'Where did you find it?' Evie asked, unable to remove her eyes from the jewel.

'The moment I read that letter, I knew exactly what Kathy meant. My mother wore this on her wedding day. It was in the safety deposit box at the bank.'

Evie thought back to the grainy photograph Hassan had found of Kathy on her wedding day and remembered the pendant that stood out against her wedding dress.

But how had it made its way back to Kathy? They'd probably never know for sure whether or not Kathy had actually sent the sapphire to Safia, but that didn't matter to Evie at the moment.

'Gran,' Evie said, coming over to her chair and putting her arm around her shoulder. Gran placed her hand on top of Evie's and looked at her, her eyes bleary. Evie wasn't sure she'd ever felt such gratitude towards anyone, and struggled to find the words to express it. 'Thank you.' Gran just smiled and put the pendant back in the envelope. 'Oh, just so you know,' Evie added, 'Maryam's grandmother hasn't read the final letter.'

'So it will be a surprise then,' Gran said with a wink.

Just then, the doorbell went. Evie slid down the corridor in her socks and opened the front door. There stood Maryam, her mother, holding a big platter of yellow biscuits with little seeds in them, and her grandmother, in pink, flowered Pakistani clothes, a puffy coat and running trainers. They lingered on the doorstep a moment until it occurred to Evie to invite them in. They each instantly took their shoes off at the door. Maryam's mum and grandma stood in the foyer, their eyes wandering into the sitting room, across the walls and back to the kitchen.

Mum came down the stairs and took their coats, and Evie led them into the kitchen, where Gran stood in front of the dining room table, her hands formally clasped behind her back. Evie noticed that she was composed, back to her usual stoic self.

'Oh, you brought biscuits,' she said, taking them from Maryam's mum. 'You needn't have done that.' Evie thought it sounded like a reprimand.

'It was no trouble,' Maryam's mum replied, undeterred. 'I'm Rezia,' she said, smiling and extending her hand, 'and this is my mother, Shehenaz.' Maryam's grandmother nodded and smiled. A shiver went down Evie's spine at hearing the name of Safia's little daughter.

Gran shook the offered hand in her no-nonsense way and said, 'Susannah. It's a pleasure,' and then walked to the far end of the table and began pouring the tea. Evie noticed that Gran had found a sort of jumper for the teapot that she didn't realise they owned.

They all took seats and sat in silence for a moment, sipping their tea, each family munching their own biscuits.

Mum broke the silence. 'So, this is really something, isn't it?'

'It really is a small world,' Maryam's mother said. Each of the women looked at their own mothers, as if urging them to say something. Then, more silence, which Evie was starting to find unbearable. She took one of the biscuits that Maryam's mum had brought and bit into it, bumping up against a bitter little seed that she tried to discreetly spit into her napkin. She glanced at Maryam, who was fiddling anxiously with her fingers. When Evie thought she couldn't take it any more, Gran spoke.

'We are, in a strange way, cousins.' Everyone snapped to at her voice, but she directed this comment at Maryam's grandmother. 'See, my mother didn't have any siblings, and I don't either. Safia was the closest she had to a sister.'

Gran was so interested in her genealogy – researching old records to map out the past ten generations – that it surprised Evie to hear her include a near-stranger in this family.

'Amma did not have any sisters either. And nor do I. So yes, cousins.' Maryam's grandmother reached across the table, extending her arm fully, to clasp Gran's hand. Evie's grandmother's expression was startled, but then she smiled and inched her hand forward.

'So, I understand from Evie that you haven't seen the final letter yet,' Gran said matter-of-factly. She put her reading glasses on, found the page in her stack, and handed it to Maryam's grandmother, who squinted at it.

'I can't make this out without my glasses,' she said, handing it to Maryam's mum. 'Read it to me, please.'

Maryam's mum began to read, and when she got to the part about the pendant, her voice caught in her throat. She looked at Gran, then Mum, then tried to go back to reading normally. When she'd finished, she put the letter down and looked from her own mum to the other people around the table, not sure what to make of it.

Without saying anything further, Gran took the pendant out of the envelope and handed it over to Maryam's grandmother.

'It's yours,' she said. 'She wanted you to have it.'

Maryam's mum put her arm between her own mother

and the jewel, as if it was dangerous, and immediately began to protest, but Maryam's grandmother just stared down at the stone in disbelief.

'We can't possibly accept this,' Maryam's mum said.

'Mum—' Evie's mum said in a low voice. Evie looked from Gran to Mum and back again.

'Helen,' Gran calmly interrupted her. 'I have thought about it, if that's what you are going to say.' Mum sat back in her chair as if that was exactly what she was going to say.

'And you,' Gran said, turning to Maryam's mum, 'simply must take it. I'm not having it back – it's not right-fully mine. So, do what you want with it, but it is yours.' She spoke with such finality that Maryam's mum went silent and drew her arm back. She stared at the glittering jewel, which Gran had put on the table between them, then looked at Maryam's grandmother, who smiled a small smile. Tears came to Maryam's mum's eyes and she dabbed at them with a napkin.

'It's OK,' Maryam's grandmother whispered. Then she said something in another language.

'I'm so sorry,' Maryam's mum said, smiling through

her tears. 'It's just that we needed some good luck right now.' Evie looked across at Maryam, who met her eyes and smiled.

Gran said, 'Well in that case, I'll take it to a jeweller to sell it this afternoon. It sounds like that might be what's needed, and it will be easier if I do it, as no one will question that it's mine.'

Evie gasped involuntarily. She hadn't thought about the jewel needing to be sold, but of course it would. She looked at the deep, shimmering blue stone surrounded by diamonds and thought it was one of the most beautiful things she'd ever seen. She thought of how long it had been with her family, through five generations – from Britain, to India, and back to Britain again. It just seemed wrong to sell it, especially since Gran hadn't even asked why they needed the money.

As if reading her thoughts, Gran turned to her and said, 'An insurance policy, remember? And now it's time to cash it in.'

They sat for a few moments, beaming at each other and looking stunned. Then Gran seemed to pick up the conversation where she'd left it before the others arrived.

'I thought I knew my mother, but I didn't at all,' she said, as if to herself. Mum looked at her in perplexed silence. Evie wondered if Gran had forgotten they had guests over.

Maryam's grandmother, who had barely said a word since entering the house and was staring intently at her biscuit, perked up. 'Me neither!' she said. 'She never let us see how brave she was. She was, in a way, a revolutionary. I believe your mother was too.'

Evie's gran nodded her agreement. 'Yes. But to us, they were just Mum.'

'They were good at that as well,' Maryam's grandmother said. The two of them looked at each other for a moment.

'I'm so glad to have met you, Shehenaz,' Gran said. Evie didn't often hear Gran speak like that – just positive, without a hint of bitterness or sarcasm. 'You don't expect to stumble upon such a discovery at this stage of life, do you?'

'No,' Maryam's grandmother agreed. 'But you should never stop hoping for surprises in life. I have learned that.'

'You know, my mother played chess her whole life. She

had such a quick mind – she could see five moves ahead. *She* would have figured this out in a minute!'

Evie's mum reached over and rubbed her back. Evie felt proud that they'd put all of this together. It made her feel like she had a bit of Kathy's quickness in her.

'Yes, my amma was the cleverest one in our family – except for Maryam, of course,' she said with a glance at her granddaughter. 'Everyone looked to her for answers, always.'

The two women bounced off each other like pinballs, sort of having a conversation, but also going in their own directions, spouting out their own feelings and realisations, so happy to unload them. In the space of a few minutes, they had exchanged their big discoveries and moved onto their own mothers' quirks and personalities. Kathy's penchant for sweets. Safia's fierce temper.

Evie smiled and shrugged at Maryam across the table, who looked back and mouthed 'Grandma Summit'. After a few more minutes, Evie jerked her head to the right to signal that she and Maryam should leave the table.

'I think they're OK without us,' Evie said, as they went down the hall. As she began to round the bannister and head upstairs with Maryam, she checked her phone and saw a text from Zoe.

Zoe: Why can't I come over now?

Evie quickly texted back.

Evie: U just can't. Tell u l8r.

Maryam glanced down at the phone and Evie put it back in her pocket.

'What was that?' Maryam asked, the smile fading from her face.

'Oh, it was just Zoe,' Evie muttered quickly. 'I'll get back to her later.' But Maryam's face had changed, and she paused at the foot of the stairs and shifted her weight from one foot to the other.

'Actually, we should just go,' she said, looking back towards the kitchen.

'Wait, what?' Evie asked. 'What's wrong?' But she suspected Maryam had seen the text, and maybe had seen the ones above, in which Evie had said she was seeing her gran, with no mention of Maryam. Even so, was it such a big deal? Maryam surely couldn't expect her to just tell her friends that they were hanging out, could she?

'It's fine. You should hang out with your real friends.

We figured out what was in the folders, so . . .' She trailed off with a shrug and turned away. Evie told her to wait, but it sounded weak coming out of her mouth and Maryam was already walking back through the kitchen, telling her mum that they probably should be going.

Maryam's mum and grandma looked confused, but took the hint, pushing back their chairs and saying that the time had flown and they really must be going.

'So soon?' Mum said. She cast Evie a questioning glance, and Evie put up her hands to show she wasn't sure what had gone wrong. Evie's gran, looking disappointed, exchanged phone numbers with Maryam's mum.

Maryam thanked Mum and Gran and said, 'See you at school,' to Evie, without looking her in the eyes, as she walked out.

Once they had left, Mum turned to Evie with a puzzled look on her face. 'What happened there?' she asked.

Once again, Evie shrugged. But the truth was, she did know what had happened. Maryam thought that Evie was ashamed of her, and was hiding their friendship from her other friends. And the truth was, she was sort of right.

27. The End of Holiday

Zoe sat on the teal bean bag, scrolling through her phone, looking for a specific song she wanted to play for Evie. It was the last week of the school holidays. Christmas and New Year had passed, and there was a lazy, restless feeling in the air – a mixture of dread and boredom. Evie sat on her bed, waiting patiently. She appreciated Zoe's dedication to knowing about music, and relied on her to pass on knowledge of whatever was new and cool. Zoe navigated the screen with one hand and brushed her dark fringe from her eyes with the other, looking for a playlist she'd made earlier. At the moment she was really into grime, most of it from a time before they were born.

'Here it is,' she said, and played the song through her phone, which, despite sounding slightly tinny, had a deep and fast baseline. Evie tried to pick up the lyrics, but couldn't make out many words.

'What's it about?' she asked.

'Like, living in a council flat and having violence all around you, I think,' she said. 'I searched it up online and I think it's about British society being unequal and racist.'

'Oh,' Evie replied lamely. She appreciated Zoe's honesty that she'd had to look it up to understand it, but she was sure Maryam would have had some choice comments about this whole scene if she was here. Evie hadn't seen her since the Grandma Summit, and imagined her like a ghost, floating around the room, quipping, 'There are some council flats where people *don't* get stabbed, you know.'

Zac and Hector burst into the room and started flossing, although Hector couldn't quite master it and kept stopping, looking at Zac and trying to copy his movements. There was no song, in Zac's opinion, that didn't call for flossing. Evie had to admit that the beat made her want to move, and she looked at Zoe, who giggled and got up, bouncing and nodding, reading the lyrics off her phone and trying to say the words along with the track.

There were loads of swear words in it, and Evie suddenly felt like she shouldn't be exposing the boys to that kind of language. She turned down the volume and ushered them out.

'I don't think my parents will like that in the house,' Evie said with a laugh.

'Mine don't mind,' Zoe said casually. 'My mum said that she likes that I'm learning about social issues through music. Like, society is actually really unfair, you know?' She scrolled through her phone for the next song. 'We're going to the anti-racism march next weekend,' she said without looking up.

'Yeah?' Evie said. She wondered if Zoe actually cared about racism. Evie imagined ghost Maryam floating around again, saying 'Posh people love to march about stuff.' Now Hassan floated into her imagination too, adding, 'Especially racism, innit.' Evie tried to shake them out of her head.

'Do you ever feel weird about, like . . .' Evie paused, trying to find the words for what she meant, 'how our friends are all basically like us?'

'What do you mean?' Zoe asked.

329

'Well, like, our parents all know each other,' she said. 'But also, we all live in the same sort of houses, and we all do the same sort of stuff.' Evie was conscious she wasn't articulating her thoughts well. It wasn't about any particular house or activity. It was that they were friends because their parents got along, and their parents got along because they were, well, quite similar. They'd all gone to university, they all made enough money, and they all liked making jokes about things they'd seen in the news. But she had trouble summing this up for Zoe in the moment. She wasn't sure she even knew what her issue with it was.

Zoe furrowed her brow defensively. 'Well, it's not our fault we get on with each other, is it? There are some people we have more in common with than others.' Her face brightened into a mischievous smirk. 'Besides,' she said, 'you're friends with *Mogyam* now, aren't you? After being partners on your project?'

There was a teasing note in this question that Evie could tell she was expected to laugh along with, but instead she flinched. How did Zoe know that she'd been seeing Maryam? Had people been talking about it? She suddenly felt suffocated, like she couldn't keep dodging what she knew was the right thing to do.

'Yes, I actually am,' she said. Then she wondered if this was true – if Maryam was indeed still her friend. 'Look, I know I came up with that nickname, but please don't make fun of her.'

Zoe looked chastened. 'Sorry,' she said. 'I didn't mean to be rude.' She went back to her phone, but then looked up. 'Hey, want to invite her over?'

Evie considered this proposal. She wanted to show Maryam that she really did want to be friends. And plus, Maryam and Zoe might actually like each other, if given the chance – they were both brilliant artists and quite funny. But something made her pause. Following on from the conversation they'd just had, it didn't feel right. It felt like Maryam was being invited because Zoe wanted to make a point.

So she said, 'Let's do it next time,' and Zoe said OK and went back to her phone to put on another fast, thumping track. Evie got up and closed the door to keep the boys and her parents out before bouncing around, stabbing the air with her hand as she pretended to know the words.

*

The next morning, Evie puttered around her room, reading a few pages of one book, then another, but unable to get into anything due to the knot of dread growing in her belly as she waited for Bella and her mum to pick them up to go to the farmers market. The thought of seeing Bella was piercing her holiday bubble, reminding her of the cat food and the awkward presentation on the last day of term. This strange break had taken her out of her normal life, but she felt normalcy clawing back at her door.

It was a soft knock, rather than clawing, that came as Mum poked her head in. 'Almost time to go,' she said. She had her big tote bag with her and was wearing what she called her 'social tracksuit' – a designer sweatshirt and yoga leggings.

'Ohhhh kaaaaay,' Evie said with a sigh, lifting her body as if it weighed a tonne.

'Well, I'm sorry going to the farmers market for a hot chocolate is *such a chore*,' Mum said sarcastically.

'It's not,' Evie admitted. She'd almost said, 'It's not *that*,' but stopped herself. She wanted to tell Mum about how awful Bella had been, how she wasn't any kind of role model, how she actually *feared* they'd be friends for life. But then again, Bella's mum was one of Mum's best friends. They weren't going to stop seeing the Underhills any time soon. There didn't seem to be any way *not* to be friends with Bella. But then Evie remembered how Mum had acted on the train after learning that 'Sarah' was Maryam. She hadn't been angry – she'd been sad, and understanding.

'Mum?' Evie said, making a snap decision. Mum, who had left the room, came back in. 'The truth is . . .' She faltered, and her mum's eyes filled with concern. 'It's that I feel sort of . . . weird around Bella lately.'

Mum exhaled, and Evie thought she saw a note of relief on her face. She came in and sat down on the bed. 'Why?'

Now it was Evie's turn to take a breath. She wasn't sure where to start. 'Well,' she said, 'for one, she's mean to Maryam. Like, she put a stack of cat food on her desk in form time the other day.'

Mum wrinkled her brow in confusion. 'Cat food . . . ?'

'Oh, right,' Evie said, backing up. 'Remember the time Maryam hissed at Bella? Well, that started this whole joke that she was like a cat. Actually, I came up with the nickname Mogyam, but that was before I even knew her, and I didn't expect it to catch on . . .' Evie trailed off, feeling that her main point was starting to get lost.

'Anyways, that's part of it, but also, Bella's just sort of . . . mean. You know?'

Evie's mum looked at her and nodded. 'I do think I know,' she said seriously. 'I've suspected something was up. And what about Zoe?'

Evie thought for a moment. 'Zoe's OK, actually. Like, sometimes she joins in with the mean stuff, but she doesn't start it, and when I ask her to stop, she does.'

Mum was quiet. She seemed to be working out what to do. But eventually, she asked, 'What do you want me to do? Should we cancel with Kate and Bella this morning?'

Evie hadn't actually thought as far as what she wanted from her mum. She realised that she'd mostly wanted to get things off her chest, and now that she had, she felt better. 'I don't think so,' she answered. 'I don't want to make it awkward. I just wanted you to know that we might not be . . . friends for life.'

Mum drew her in for a hug, speaking into the top of her head. 'Oh, Evie. Dad and I are just scared of getting it wrong now that you're in secondary school. We thought your old friends would be a comfort.' She drew back and looked Evie in the face. 'But you can decide who your real friends are. You know, the way you and Maryam tracked down and then solved those letters together, it was amazing to watch. You've got good taste in people, Evie.' She gave Evie a kiss and walked out, telling her to remember her gloves.

28. Mutton for Six

Maryam and her mum walked up the high street market, navigating the stalls, which was made more difficult by the wheelie bag her mum dragged behind her.

'Do you *need* to bring that thing?' Maryam asked with exasperation. The wheelie bag made Maryam want to die of shame, but Mum seemed immune to embarrassment.

'What's wrong? It makes the shopping so much easier to carry home,' Mum said. Maryam rolled her eyes and pulled her scarf up around her mouth to trap her warm breath. It was a very grey and very cold day, and it felt like it needed to snow. The miserable weather meant the market was less busy than usual, so they could walk down the street easily, Mum's wheelie bag, full of potatoes and onions, jittering along the cobblestones.

They had one more stop, the halal butcher. Whole skinned and gutted sheep hung upside down in the window. Mum started chatting to the man behind the counter and Maryam gazed out the glass door. She heard Mum order half a dozen cow's feet and three mutton shanks. Maryam watched coat-covered strangers, all with hoods up or hats on, hustle past as little bits of wet, sloppy snow started to fall.

Two such coat-covered figures ran under the red awning of the butcher to get cover from the sleet. She saw them pointing at the red flesh of the headless sheep with disgust and realised, horrified, that they were Evie and Arabella. She hadn't spoken to Evie since she'd left her house over a week ago, although Mum and Nani had met with Evie's gran to sort out the money.

She felt a weird combination of gratitude and anger and shame. Part of her couldn't believe that she'd walked out on Evie. Wasn't a friend exactly what she wanted right now – *especially* a friend who had helped to save her family's business? But it wasn't enough, it turned out. You couldn't be friends with someone who wouldn't admit they were friends with you, who didn't stand up to anyone who was awful to you. That kind of friend couldn't be on your side – not really, anyway.

Maryam had been running this justification through her mind for the past few days, convincing herself and burying the thought of ever having to return to school and share a table with Evie. She couldn't imagine anyone she'd less like to run into than Evie and Arabella, *together.*

Arabella covered her mouth with her hand, laughing and making an expression of revulsion at the sheep carcass, which dangled headlessly behind her. Evie teased her, making a face that could only have been a dead sheep. Their mothers also looked at the sheep and then at each other, disgusted.

Maryam turned back into the shop, moving towards her mother, and found that she was positioning the two white bags of meat safely inside her bag before zipping it up. Maryam looked around the freezing shop desperately, hoping there was something else they needed so they wouldn't have to leave.

'OK, let's go,' Mum said, fishing out her umbrella.

'Don't you think we should wait in here until it stops

dumping down?' Maryam said, hoping at the same time that Evie and Bella would just move off.

'Don't be silly,' Mum said. 'We're not just going to wait in the butcher's. Besides, it doesn't look like it's stopping anytime soon.'

Mum was right. The sleet was getting heavier, turning into snow. Maryam exhaled in defeat. She put her hood up and made a plan: if she turned sharply to the left out of the shop, she hoped she could avoid being seen by Evie and Arabella, who stood to the right of the door. She let her mum go first like a test balloon, holding the door for her, and seeing her turn left without being noticed. The test was successful. Maryam put her hood up and slipped out behind her mum. It was at that moment that Evie, Arabella and their mothers decided to move off and brave the weather, and crossed in front of the shop doorway. Maryam, her vision blocked by her big, fur-trimmed hood, ploughed directly into Arabella.

'Sorry,' she said, before registering what had happened. She looked up to see Arabella's face full of disdain.

'Hey, watch it,' Arabella said, but then did a double take when she realised it was Maryam. Wordlessly, she narrowed her green eyes and turned to walk away. But Evie, who was right behind, noticed her and stopped.

'Maryam, hi!' she said, seeming genuinely happy to see her.

'Oh, hey,' Maryam said flatly. She had been nursing her grievances over the past week, building up her hurt, remembering all the times Evie had failed to acknowledge her in public despite them having such a special connection. But now that she saw her, smiling as if nothing had happened, she felt less angry than awkward.

Evie's mum also said hello to Maryam, and then, noticing her mum, said, 'Rezia!' and gave her a hug. She introduced Ms Underhill, who looked desperate to break away.

'How is everything?' Evie asked Maryam while their mothers chatted. 'Is it all OK with the shop now?'

Maryam snuck a glance at Arabella, who was looking at the space next to Maryam's head as if she wasn't there at all.

'Yeah, it's all OK for now. Thanks again,' she added awkwardly. 'But Hassan and I are still writing a letter to the council to see if they can limit how much landlords raise rents. Maybe some of your parents and their friends could sign?' Maryam hadn't planned to ask, but it just came tumbling out.

'Sure, I bet they would. Hey, Mum—' Evie started, but Ms Underhill cut in.

'It's very nice to meet you, but we really must be getting out of this weather,' she said briskly, and turned to leave. Evie's mum said goodbye, and that they must catch up sometime soon, and they all started to move off. Maryam felt the tension in her body dissipate. Good, it was over, and it hadn't gone too badly.

'Oh, one more thing,' Evie said, turning back and making Maryam tense up again. 'I just wanted to say I'm sorry. You know, for not being a good friend.'

She spoke loudly, so everyone could hear. Through the bits of snow that had melted into droplets on the lenses of her glasses, Maryam cast a glance at Arabella, who had one nostril wrinkled, like she'd smelled a bad smell. Maryam could see what Evie was doing – she was making a point. Maryam looked from Arabella back to Evie, who gave her an earnest look, as if to say *really, I mean it.*

It was what Maryam had needed her to do all along

– admit they were friends. She smiled a closed-mouth smile and nodded her appreciation of the gesture.

'Do you want to hang out this weekend?' Evie went on. 'You could give me that letter you'd like the parents to sign.'

'Sure,' Maryam said hesitantly. For an alarming moment she thought Evie might invite Arabella too, but she didn't. She hadn't realised she would feel so relieved to make it up with Evie, or how little it would take to do it. 'Maybe you could come over to mine this time,' she said, surprising herself.

'Sure,' Evie said. She glanced at Arabella, as if to make sure she was still paying attention.

'Lunch tomorrow?' Maryam proposed, as if it was normal. Evie looked to her mum, who nodded her assent.

They said goodbye, and Maryam and her mum turned up the street, the wheelie bag struggling on the snowy pavement. Maryam's mind wandered to what on earth they could cook for a guest – Evie was the only person she could remember inviting over for lunch who wasn't a relative.

Turning to Mum, Maryam asked with a hint of

mischief, 'Is there enough mutton for Evie? I think she liked the look of that sheep in the window.'

They cackled, and Mum, pulling her scarf over her head, said, 'Oh, yes. You can always make the *nihari* stretch for one more.' Maryam smiled. Cooked down with spices into a warm, rich, gravy, Evie would see that it was delicious. They trudged up the slushy pavement, and Maryam took the handle of the wheelie bag from Mum and forced it over the cracks. Her heart felt light in the dreary weather – it was a new year, and as she marched past the bare trees and through the freezing puddles, she felt excited for tomorrow.

Acknowledgments

This book would not have been good enough to put into the world without the brilliant feedback of my first reader, Freya. You are a froggy wise beyond your years. I'm also grateful to my other brilliant readers – Isla Abernethy, the McNallys, the Falik-Pasternacks, and the Heiges clan – who lent me their keen eyes and kind words.

Of course, thank you to my parents, to whom this book is dedicated. My mother taught me to read, but more than that, she is a great watcher who taught me to notice people. She helped me to see the nuance in the world, with all its awkward social dynamics and complicated characters. My father is a doer more than a watcher, with a remarkable life story that he talks about too little. I'm sure I could fill books with what I still don't know about it. I was honored to borrow a small bit of his history for this book.

Thank you to Neil, who has always believed that I'm good at this, and who not only encouraged me, but showed he meant it by working harder so I could go part-time and write. He helped me have the proverbial room of my own – no small feat when raising three children. He is more of an artist than he tends to admit, and I'm so lucky to have him.

Thank you to Nico, my model of a brilliant and beloved younger brother, and Penny, my model of a bold and brave girl.

Thank you to Kevan. Every time I write a great brother it's because I have one.

Thank you to all of the amazing women who I'm lucky enough to call friends – you know who you are. Your honesty, fortitude, humour, irreverence, and faith in me matters more than you will ever know. I hope our kids have this.

Thank you to Bella, who took a chance on me and helped my lifelong dream come true. I am forever grateful. The exceptional team at Guppy saw what I was trying to do and helped me to do that thing a little better. Thank you to Hannah, for her hawk eyes and subtle solutions, and to Catherine, for being the world's best publicist.

Thank you to Paula, whose favourite character is Hassan (he's mine too).

Thank you to the academics – Rotem Geva at the Hebrew University of Jerusalem and Stephen Legg at the University of Nottingham – who were so generous in giving me thoughtful feedback on how I depicted 1930s Delhi. And thank you to another expert, Safia Javed, who taught me the Qur'an when I was a young girl and gave me insights from her family about the time and place I was trying to conjure. She has always been a figure of generosity in our family's life; I hope my character does her name justice.

Thank you to Rachel Hamilton, whose early edits and encouragement were so valuable, and to Adamma Okonkwo, whose Golden Egg sessions were a joy. Thank you also to all of the published writers who chose to help me before I was one.

Finally, thank you to the melting pot of London, where all of our different selves have a home. You are a beautiful, magical place. This story is about you more than anyone.